A Tale of Two Lilies

Dr. Dibyendu Pal

 pencil

ISBN 978-93-5458-282-0
© Dr. Dibyendu Pal 2021
Published in India 2021 by Pencil

A brand of
One Point Six Technologies Pvt. Ltd.
123, Building J2, Shram Seva Premises,
Wadala Truck Terminal, Wadala (E)
Mumbai 400037, Maharashtra, INDIA
E connect@thepencilapp.com
W www.thepencilapp.com

DISCLAIMER: *This is a work of fiction. Names, characters, places, events and incidents are the products of the author's imagination. The opinions expressed in this book do not seek to reflect the views of the Publisher.*

Author biography

**************** ***************** ****************
****

Dr. Dibyendu Pal was an eminent Chemical Engineer during his service life. He is also a poet & litterateur. He dedicated his retired life in the field of literature. His poems, articles, short stories in Bengali & English languages have been published in various news papers, Global Anthology (Heaven) and Asian Anthology. Several novels have been published in both Bengali & English languages. Dr. Dibyendu Pal is honoured as an Executive Member of the Governing Body of Michael Madhusudan Academy, Kolkata.

CONTENTS

Foreword

Caption

Preface

A TALE OF TWO LILIES

Preface:

We heard about the birth of water lily from clay.

In this way two buds of water lily took birth in the clayey water. Thereafter several days passed. These buds began to be blooming within the polluted atmosphere. And once they opened their smiling face towards the sun. The fragrance of lotus floated in the air but didn't get the opportunity to behold that clay-born lotus. The butterfly smelling the aroma of white & red lotus reached to make boon companionship with it. But unfortunately, we couldn't go near her to open our heart expressing our fondness to her.

The human being may take birth in the indigent domestic life. But alike lotus he or she may arise as a superhuman or a man/woman with supernatural power due to dominance of will-force. The wave of his or her fragrance, her effulgence, her scintillation, her infallible humanity spreads all over the world. In one case, the gloomy lives of the countless patients were illuminated by the inundation of beam of light.

Human life is mortal. But the mortality of human

beings can be transformed into immortality through the performance of good & virtuous deeds. The credentials, the milestone of the glorious deeds of this celebrated person are being appeared in the world with the rising head.

Now, I will narrate the life stories of two great women, who beside all the obstructions, they achieved the lime light in life due to their will force and endless endeavour.

Dedication

Dedicated to
My loving
Mother
&
Readers

Yellow Butterfly

<u>1st Chapter</u>

It is dawn. At the northeastern nook floating array of white clouds is being painted with crimson red by the rays of the rising sun. Somewhere from a distant place, some wildfowl is singing the welcome song of dawn in an elevated tune. The just awakened flock of birds replete the atmosphere with their melodious chirping. An easterly gentle breeze carries the song of invocation of the sun. Flower buds blossom to receive the stream of rays of crimson sun opening their smiling petals. Black bumblebees fly with a low humming noise. Honeybees are seen flying in search of nectar. Black bees for pollination fly from flowers to flowers. Butterflies arrive in swarm extending their colorful wings. The whistling of grasshoppers, crowing of cocks, barking of dogs, the mooing of cows bring the message of dawn. A colorful conversation begins among flowers in the flower garden. Being smeared with the pleasant touch of color dawn she comes. Floating in the surging rippling youthful billows she comes. She comes with gentle & slow steps like the silent fall of dew. She comes in a yellow Shari & striped yellow blouse. Her disheveled curling hair looks like the waving black sea. Her face seems to be a quiet disposition of the lifeless portrait of Monalisa.

She comes with a face hung down in shyness, carrying a small yellow bag in her hand. During this colorful fair of dawn, this Yellow Butterfly is also a participant. Yes, I named her Yellow Butterfly.

No, she is not a paragon of beauty. She is not a fairy. Rather, she is dark-complexioned. Her face has some lax beauty. A small round yellow paint put on her forehead. She walks with a flamingo gait.

Yellow Butterfly comes. She comes daily along with the birds chirping on the trees. Sitting on the terrace I drink the essence of colorful dawn.

That girl occasionally glances at me with her large shy eyes. At the exchange of sight, she bends her face bashfully. In exchange for daily sight grows a distant friendship. Sometimes the smiling face of Yellow Butterfly reflects the cheerfulness. She is a regular passerby but where is her destination? I become inquisitive about her destination. I desire to know where she goes floating in the inundation of splendorous dawn.

It comes to know that Yellow Butterfly works as a nurse-maid giving service to an octogenarian old woman. Taking care & serving that old woman throughout the day, she returns home after sunset.

The day after day passes. Daily I happen to see Yellow Butterfly. Once, that exchange of speechless silent smiles comes towards an end. My Yellow Butterfly while returning to her home says waving her hand, "Goodbye uncle. I am leaving today", I replied, "Be happy. God bless you." The girl leaves with a sweet smile.

2nd Chapter

So many months passed. The sun rises & paints the array of clouds with crimson red. The chirping of birds resounds in the air & sky. Flowers blossom in the garden. The black humble-bees sing with a low humming sound. Honey-bees fly. The colorful butterflies take part in the colorful fair of flowers. Only does not come to that large-eyed bashful Yellow Butterfly.

Turning around & round every year begins the Kolkata Bookfair. By the invitation of the Bookfair committee Guild, several publishers gather at the fair. Every year the book fair is decorated with some particular theme. The various bookstalls are decorated with colorful lightings. It's not that in this book fair only books are traded. An ample arrangement is made for the entertainment of book lovers & the public. Numbers of savory eatables & sweet shops come to the fair to satiate the tongues of fair comers. Many tea & coffee shops install their shops. On the premises of the book fair, various cultural activities are arranged in the evening.

Every year I attend this book fair as a lover of books. Walking around from bookstalls to stalls I become engaged in purchasing books.

Last few years I couldn't be present at the book fair since I was busy publishing several novels.

After so many years I was informed about the conduction of the Kolkata book fair in the month of December. For a long, I couldn't go to Bookfair. Hence at the appearance of the month of December, I couldn't but plunge into the Bookfair, not as a spectator but as a book lover.

While loitering near the various bookstalls, toying with the colorful books, a precious book comes to my notice, "VEDAS – THE ULTIMATE VOICE OF THE UNIVERSE". Taking out the book from the rack, observing its colorful cover page, I read the name of the author of the book. He is Dr, Bidhan Datta, a renowned poet & litterateur. Purchasing this book as I handed over the price of the book to the publisher's representative, a female voice emitted from my side, *"Uncle you are here! Can you recognize me?"*

Being struck dumb I look at the girl. A smart girl, large eyes, black curled hair disheveled up to the waist, wearing colorful Shalwar & Kurta. The face of the girl seems to be very familiar to me. Who is this girl? She is addressing me as 'uncle'. Perhaps she knows me. Seeing me gazing at her steadfastly she says, *"Certainly you can't recognize me. Is it not uncle? Can you recollect, a few years back at dawn I used to pass in front of your house to serve an old lady as a nursemaid?"*

In an instant, the door of my memory gets unlocked. Affectionately I say, *"Oh yes! I could get it now. You are my Yellow Butterfly."*
"Yellow Butterfly! Why Yellow Butterfly uncle?' She asks astonishingly.
I explain, *"During dawn when the crimson red sun rays paint the array of clouds, you used to come with your bright yellow Shari to join the colorful fair of nature. That's why I named you Yellow Butterfly."* The girl now says giggling, *"Uncle really you are a person of a contemplative turn of mind. I think you are a poet. Is it not uncle?"*

"Oh Noh. Nothing of that sort. I liked you going with your yellow Shari during that colorful dawn that's why I denominated you

as Yellow Butterfly. By the bye what's your good name?"

"Shabnam. Shabnam Mondal."

"What a sweet name! Do you know the meaning of Shabnam?"

"Yes, uncle. Dew of dawn"

"Excellent! Excellent! You are correct. Shabnam means Dew of dawn. What a coincidental conjunction! The particles of dew silently drop from the sky of dawn. And at that moment another dew dot Shabnam comes with silent steps to mingle her yellow color with the colorful nature. What a wonderful conjunction! Is it not Shabnam?"

"This wonderful simile is possible for you only. You are a great poet, that's why every event becomes poetic art in your inward eyes. I am an ordinary girl. I don't know so much. But no doubt your imaginative power is praiseworthy."

"Leave it. You need not admire me. Come on; let us sit somewhere to chat."

"That's good. Let us take the seat in the nearby restaurant."

Along with Shabnam, I sit in a nearby restaurant.

"Now tell me Shabnam what you like to eat?"

"No uncle. Nothing. I have already had lunch."

"You came out of your house in the early morning. Certainly, you are hungry now. Take something eatable now. We will talk while eating."

"Then please order for tea only."

"No. Not tea alone. I will ask for a fish cutlet."

Calling the waiter I order two cups of tea & two plates of fish cutlets. While consuming the eatable & drink Shabnam says, *"Uncle I really like your naming me as Yellow Butterfly."*

"Your Shabnam name is too sweet. But, Shabnam, your presence in this book fair indicates that you are fond of purchasing & reading the books. Is it not?"

"Yes, uncle. You can say I am a bookworm. That's why I come to this book fair every year."

"What types of books you like to read?"

"On the whole, all types of books are my favorite. But I prefer mostly the educative & mythological books."

"OK, I understand your liking for the educative book. But why is your inclination towards mythological books?"

"Since, in general, the peoples think mythologies as imaginary fables of poets only. But I try to search from these ancient scriptures the ancient history, ancient social systems, manners & customs, the art of warfare, etc."

"That's true. It's impractical to let lose these mythologies as imaginary fables. Each & every mythology or epic has some true anecdotes or history concealed in it."

"Yes uncle, whether it is Ramayana or Mahabharata or Purans of India, or Ancient Greek epics by Homer the Iliad, Odyssey; Whether it is Old Testament, Arabian Nights or epic of Gilgamesh every one conceals the ancient unknown history of that place. That's why I prefer these books and purchase whenever get an opportunity."

"That's a good habit. I am astonished! Have you gone through these precious books?"

"Yes, uncle. I will bring out the truth of these epics one by one. Some people were of opinion that Lord Shri Krishna of Mahabharata was an imaginary hero. But after the discovery of Shri Krishna's kingdom 'Dwaravati' under the gulf near Dwarka of Gujarat the truthfulness of the epic Mahabharata has been revealed. Today or tomorrow truthfulness of the epic Ramayana will also be revealed. Some of the disbelievers mockingly say that there was nobody like Rama. Even they disregard Adam's bridge between India & Shri Lanka as a naturally evolved. But Nasa's satellite survey indicated that the bridge was manmade and of about 7000 years old. Gradually several pieces of evidence are coming out about the truthfulness of Ram & Sita's episode. The epic Iliad & Odyssey by Homer has already revealed the history of ancient Greek."

"What's about the story of Gilgamesh? Is it true?"

"Certainly, true uncle. The Epic story of Gilgamesh was discovered in the ruins of the library of Ashurbanipal in Nineveh by Hormuzd Rassam in 1853. Written in cuneiform on 12 clay tablets, this Acadian version dates from around 1300 to 1000 B.C. This oldest epic tale in the world was written 1500 years before Homer wrote the Iliad."

"What more you know about this Gilgamesh epic?"

"'The Epic of Gilgamesh' conveys many themes important to our understanding of Mesopotamia and its kings. Themes of friendship, the role of the king, enmity, immortality, death, male-female relationships, city versus rural life, civilization versus the wild, and relationships of humans and gods resound throughout the poem. Gilgamesh's many challenges throughout the poem serve to mature the hero and make him a good king to his people. Gilgamesh was not only an epic hero but a historical king of Uruk who appears in contemporary letter and inscriptions found by archaeologists."

"I am really surprised that you have mugged up the histories so preciously. If I am not mistaken, I think you are a student."

"Yes uncle, I am in the final year of my Master's degree at Kolkata University."

"In which subject you are studying?"

"Political science and sociology as my main subjects"

"Besides Political Science, you have a keen interest in ancient histories too. Is it not Shabnam?"

"Yes, I have."

"As far as I recollect, when you used to pass in front of my house for going to a house to look after an ailing old lady, I never thought that you were engaged in studies. Were you a student during that period? I didn't know where did you come from? I couldn't know who your family members were."

"I am from a village in Nadia district. Uncle, when you saw me *working as a nursemaid, I used to attend that old lady temporarily in place of my sick mother during that period. Two days after I left that place, that old lady expired. I couldn't go but my mother had been there to attend the funeral pyre of the lady."*

"Oh! Very sad news. But you will have to return to your village now. Are you not getting late."

"No uncle, I stay in a girl's hostel in Kolkata. Only on holidays, I go to a town near to my village."

"It is then a very tough time for you?"

"Uncle, my entire life is very tough. I have to struggle at every step of my life. Listening to my life history, you not only will be surprised but you will feel it as heart-rending."

With an amazing look, I stared at her afflicted face sometimes. Slowly I said, *"If you don't feel embarrassed you can express your struggling life episodes to me."*

"Uncle I won't be embarrassed. I'll narrate my life history since my birth. Of course, about my babyhood, I learned from my 'Ammu' (mummy). That was a very sad & struggling life."

With an afflicted voice Shabnam begins her struggling life.

<u>3rd Chapter</u>

"Nadia district - about 45 kilometers from Kolkata city. A small suburban township in this district. A remote village at some furlong away from town is of unparalleled beauty. While walking through the rural pathway several Tiled roofed cottages are noticed in rows. Within the courtyards of some of the earthen-walled cottages are found some of the domestic cows tied in the cowsheds. The cows are found to be busy chewing the cud. The path through the open field goes straight towards the river

Yamuna. Yamuna River is not that the Yamuna of ancient days. Present Yamuna River has lost itself & assumed the shape of the pond in the course of time. Even then the rural peoples call it the Yamuna River. Some of the old aged persons describe the ancient history of the Basin of Yamuna River of a very distant past. Some of the crop fields are located by the bank of the river. Paddy, wheat, maize fields are also seen. At some interior fields plantation of betel leaves is noticed. On the outskirts of this village with flourishing greenery, some fifteen Muslim families are dwelling. These indigent peoples are residing around a mosque. On minute observation their indigence can be noticed. Besides somewhat tidiness the fragilities of the huts are not of pleasing sight. The herd of dogs & goats, flock of hens are found loitering in the courtyards. Some half-necked children are found playing with wooden sticks on the rural path. There is a clear sign of want of education on their faces.

Dwellers of the majority Hindu community are not very far off from the Muslim locality. Most of them have mud-built houses with thatched Tin or tiled roofs. In the courtyards of some of them have holy basil scaffolds. Surrounding these scaffolds painted different designs with liquid rice paste. Walking a furlong away comes a palatial building made up of marble stones & bricks. This palace is bearing the history of the cultural heritage of splendor of Zamindar (Landlord) of the past. On one side of this palace, built on vast land, has a large tank. Paved wharf...dilapidated owing to the influence of time. A Lord Shiva temple & a place of worship are a little away from the palace. Still, some priest is engaged for offering puja (worship) to the deity. The descendants of Zamindar assemble in the palace during any festival arranged from one generation to another.

This poverty-stricken Muslim locality looks dissimilar abreast of the slanderous palace. Here a Muslim family resides. A small hut made of straw consists of two tiny dingy rooms... a small kitchen of wattle. A thatched cell for hen behind the courtyard... A small well at a corner of the courtyard. A resident of this hut is Muhammad Shahjahan & his Bibi (wife) Mumtaz Begum and their only male child Kader Muhammad. When the age of their only son Kader was two years, a beautiful baby was born. Since the baby took birth at the dawn of winter, the female baby was named Shabnam. Poverty-stricken parent...Abbu (Father) earns his livelihood by driving a rickshaw in the suburban area. After the birth of a female child, it became impossible to bear subsistence for the four family members. Being helpless, Mumtaz had to earn working sometimes as a laborer in the paddy field or sometimes as a mason's assistant. She had to work in the workplace tying baby Shabnam on her back. Little child Kader used to accompany his Abbu in the rickshaw.

In this way, their daily & customary struggle of life was going on. The working-class peoples may not have an abandon of wealth but there is no impediment of peace of mind & happiness. That's why there was no sign of expression of grief due to the insufficiency of money among the family of Shahjahan. There was an environment of a bit of peace in their hand-to-mouth family. There existed benediction of 'Allah' within their hearts. On every *Jummabar* (Friday) they used to attain mosque for '*Namaj*' (Mahommadan prayer) praying to almighty 'Allah" for eternal peace of mind.

But inevitable are the decrees of fate. Weal and woe come by turns as the wheel of fortune moves. Hence a startling event descended on the family of Shahjahan.

That morning of winter was enveloped by dense mist. Shahjahan was pulling his rickshaw towards the suburb. Three years old Kader was sitting in the back seat. The entire place was overcast by impenetrable fog. The roads were not visible clearly through the impervious white sheet. Shahjahan was pulling his rickshaw conjecturally towards the suburb. Unexceptionally, his rickshaw collided with a four-wheeler coming from the opposite side. Shahjahan flew up with a jerk on the road & lost his sense. He was seriously injured. Kader fell down & received a blow from the vehicle.

When Shahjahan got back his sense, he was lying on the bed of General hospital. Sitting near his head, Mumtaz was weeping incessantly. On her lap lying one-year-old Shabnam. Her child Kader was found at the spot dead.

Shabnam came to know all these events from her 'Ammu' (Mummy) later on.

Losing Kader, Shabnam became her 'Ammu's gem of eyes. Bathe, putting on clothes, dressing up, putting up collyrium on eyes 'Ammu' used to take her to the playground near the mosque. At every moment when the face of Kader appeared on her heart, Mumtaz embracing Shabnam used to burst into tears in the gushing stream. Little baby, Mumtaz Shabnam used to stare at her 'Ammu' being struck dumb.

After the death of Kader, Mumtaz didn't go for any job. Relinquishing all the jobs, she became busy nursing her child Shabnam. After discharge from the hospital, Shahjahan began pulling rickshaws after getting his rickshaw repaired. But whatever amount he earned by pulling a rickshaw, that was not sufficient to maintain his family. As such he sometimes had to work as a worker in the agricultural field of some landowner. The untimely death of Kader brought some tempestuous wind of affliction in their family. Of course, that existed momentarily. Afterward, while performing 'Namaj' in the mosque, Shahjahan perceived that whatever would happen on the earth; all are due to the will of 'Allah' To memorize that he hanged a religious verse on the thatched wall given by some 'Molla' (Muslim teacher) of the mosque."

<u>4th Chapter</u>

Saying up to this Shabnam takes out a paper inscribing the following *Bayet'* (The verse).

The *'Bayet'* (The verse) showed by Shabnam is like this.....

Bismillahi tawak-kaltu 'alal laah. Walaa haula walaa quw-wata illaa bil-laah

With Allah's name we leave. We rely on Allah. There is no strength to obtain from evil or to good except with Allah's help.

Allaahumma innii as-a-luka khairal maulaji wa khairal makhraji. Bismillaahi walajnaa wa Bismillaahi khrajnaa wa 'alal laahi rabbanaa tawak-kalnaa.

Oh, Allah, I beg of you a good admission into the home and a good exiting from me. With Allah's name do we enter and leave the home and upon Allah, our Sustainer, do we rely on.

I take the paper in my hand from Shabnam & read the English portion of it. It is really commendable that the Muslim faith in 'Allah' is so strong. I admire this. Returning the paper of verse to Shabnam I ask her to continue the story of her struggling life.

Keeping mum for a while Shabnam begins recapitulating her life story.

5th Chapter

"For establishing mental stability, it took about six months in the family of Shahjahan. In the meanwhile, once Mumtaz happened to meet with one Muslim woman, Murshida Begum by name of Muslim locality at the courtyard of the mosque. Listening to the woeful tale of Mumtaz, Murshida Begum expressed her sympathy with a heart full of sorrow. Murshida Begum advised Mumtaz to join some new job; so that besides earning money, the unexpected miserable environment in the domestic life would be alleviated. But the main problem of Mumtaz was where to keep Shabnam throughout her working period. Mumtaz was unable to decide anything. If she would take the job as a laborer under some mason or working in the agricultural field, she would have to work keeping Shabnam tied on her back. During that type of work, there is every possibility of Shabnam being involved in danger. Mumtaz spoke out her difficulty to Murshida Begum. Murshida Begum keeping silent for a while thought deeply about the problem. She assured Mumtaz that she would find out some suitable job for her. Mumtaz returned to her hut with Shabnam on her lap.

Mumtaz became engaged in her staggering domestic life. Always being deeply concerned about Shabnam, she kept busy with Shabnam. Days passed, nights arrived. Looking at the twinkling stars in the night sky Mumtaz searched for her beloved son Kader among the stars. Often she perceived that Kader was at rest on the lap of Almighty 'Allah'. Sleepless night terminated at the advent of dawn by summoning of the morning star. In this way, some more days passed. After a few weeks, Murshida Begum arrived at Mumtaz's hut. Mumtaz cordially welcomes her & took her inside the room offering her a tottering folding chair to sit on. Both the women co-sharer in suffering became absorbed in the stories of their own distress.

In the course of the conversation, Murshida Begum told Mumtaz about a lucrative job. Listening to that Mumtaz asked her what type of job that would be. Murshida explained to her that a motherly woman of mild disposition urgently required a nursery school at the nearby township to look after the babies. If Mumtaz would join the concern, there won't be any difficulty to keep Shabnam safe. Shabnam would be able to play with the other babies in the nursery. While looking after the babies along with Shabnam, Mumtaz would achieve transparent tranquillity. Listening to a detailed offer of Murshida Begum, Mumtaz anxiously said, *'I don't have any experience with this. Then how the employer will appoint me?'* Murshida Begum said with a gentle smile, 'The amount of affection you preserve for your offspring, that affection you squeeze out from your heart for the babies. That will be your competency for the job. You will look after those sweetest flowers playing with them throughout the day. You will fulfill their childish whim with a smiling face. Those little babies will forget their own parent for time being in the presence of an affectionate mother like you.'

'Are those babies orphans? Don't they have a parent?' Mumtaz became sympathetic.

'Oh no! They have. But when their parents depart for their working places, they are relieved of anxiety leaving their babies here in the nursery. That's why this nursery was created. But one important word keeps in your mind that you & Shabnam must come here wearing clean clothing & being neat & tidy. Do you agree to this?' Nodding her head, giving her consent Mumtaz said, *'In that case, please enroll my name to them. If they select me kindly intimate me Didi (Elder sister).'*

After about two weeks Mumtaz was fortunate to get an interview call from the interview board of the nursery and finally got an appointment as a caretaker of the infants of the nursery. That job of nursery turned the life of Mumtaz towards a new phase of life. While looking after the infants with motherly affection Mumtaz achieved the provision of survival. Mumtaz won the infants' hearts looking after the individual infants equally, feeding & dressing up timely, singing charming songs. Shabnam too was being grown up amongst the infants. In between different games, the infants were being acquainted with the world of education either through the various toys or colorful books of rhymes. For that nursery education, a young teacher was appointed. The name of that teacher was Sudipa Roy. The dweller of that township Sudipa was a soft-spoken graceful youth & a Montessori trained teacher. Besides Sudipa, there was a tribal woman named Yuthika Hembrome. Bulky-statured, mild disposition pious Christian Yuthika was in a real sense a person of educative mentality. Yuthika was allotted the duty of supplying different dishes to the infants to their choice. She used to sing the English nursery rhyme in a pleasant tune in front of the infants.

Months after months were passing for Mumtaz in playing & singing the rural songs amongst those innocent infants like pure flowers. The simplicity of the infants & rural simplicity of Mumtaz became amalgamated. Mumtaz could perceive the competency of education while working in the nursery. She could understand that without being enlightened in the educational enlightenment, it won't be possible to drive away from the darkness enveloping the rural educational system. That perception encouraged Mumtaz to be acquainted with the rudimentary learning, to become familiar with the colorful books fit for juvenile reading. And who extended the helping hand towards the rudimentary learning of Mumtaz was Sudipa Roy. That beam of light of nursery education illuminated the courtyard of the small hut of Mumtaz. The illiterate Rickshaw puller Shahjahan was getting the flavor of that education. He too could perceive the utility of education. Several quarries arose in the mind of Shahjahan, *'why this rural Muslim society is immersed in the darkness of illiteracy?'* Shahjahan & Mumtaz swore that they would bring up their only child Shabnam with proper education.

Education began in the life of little Shabnam. But it wasn't only for Shabnam but also for Mumtaz. With the soft touch of the sun-beam, all three of them used to get up from sleep. After completion of morning duties, all of them sit for *Namaz*. Thereafter Mumtaz & Shabnam used to engage in the studies of juvenile literature. Shahjahan tried to achieve knowledge of the alphabet. The private tutor at home for Shahjahan was Mumtaz. Thus Shahjahan was trying hard to be acquainted with the alphabet. Sitting near them, little Shabnam used to giggle silently.

The illiterate Shahjahan could find the trace of a new world of learning. He tried to perceive the meaning of the Urdu Bayet hanging on the fence of wattles, received from the mosque. He tried hard to read but being ignorant of the Urdu alphabet, unable to read. Being enlightened on the value of learning, he approached with folded hands to the *'Moulavi'* (Learned Mohammedan scholar)' of the Mosque to teach him the Urdu alphabet. He thought if he could get minimum knowledge of Urdu then he would be able to comprehend the majesty of almighty **'Allah'**.Mumtaz was too eager to learn Urdu from *'Moulavi'* but in her Muslim society, women's education was a secondary object. Mumtaz was getting knowledge of Urdu from her husband.

Thus their daily life steam was going on flowing in full swing. Shabnam was growing up along with the urban children within the premises of the nursery. Shabnam was receiving education from the teachers of various religions. Gradually Shabnam was being cognized as a talented pupil. Besides bookish education, Shabnam was becoming competent in different games, dancing, cultural activities & paintings. Observing the latent intellect of minor Shabnam, all her teachers became amazed. Mumtaz too was astonished observing the latent talent of tiny Shabnam. Mumtaz affectionately looking at Shabnam mumbles, *'which is this hoory (fairy) from Jannat (Heaven) took birth within my womb? All this is the Almighty Allah's grace.'* While floating in the current of time passed about five to six years. Shabnam now had grown up to the age of six years or so. Now she could feel the hardship of her family. She could feel the affliction of her 'Ammu'. She could perceive the financial constraint of her family. *'Can she not alleviate this hardship of her family?'* She expressed her mental distress to her 'Ammu'.

'Ammu' with a sweet smile said with a kiss on Shabnam's cheek, *'My loving child, you now concentrate on your studies more so that you can become erudite in the future. Then only you can earn much to alleviate our hardship in getting a good job.'* Shabnam listened to her Ammu patiently. Her large eyes filled with tears. She became promise-bound to continue her studies by any means to become erudite in the future so that she can alleviate the pecuniary difficulties of her family.

The years were passing through deep in studies. Shabnam had a determination that she would have to be edified through studies only. She would have to be established of her own just to alleviate the distress of her 'Ammu' & 'Abbu'. She was going on crossing the boundary lines of school successfully one after the other obtaining good results in examinations.

Higher Secondary examination was approaching fast. All hours of day & night were being spent concentrating on studies by adolescent Shabnam aged 15 years. 'Ammu' Mumtaz encouraged her daughter in between her household works. At night she preparing tea made Shabnam drink so that she shouldn't droop down in drowsiness. At dawn, Shabnam fell asleep. But Mumtaz shouldn't lie in a slumberous state. She had numerous works beside her domestic duties. She would have to go to the nursery to look after the children.

Shabnam appeared in the Higher Secondary

Examination & fared well in all the subjects securing good marks. The male & female teachers of her school liked Shabnam not only because of her excellent results in the class examinations but also because of her extracurricular activities. Shabnam was a good painter by nature. She used to participate in school dramas & sports. A versatile talented Shabnam won the hearts of every one of her schools.

Waiting with bated breath when the result of the Higher Secondary Examination was declared, it was found Shabnam passed in the first division with star marks in several subjects. The principal & all the teachers congratulated Shabnam for the excellent result. 'Ammu' Mumtaz too became very much satisfied.

So many expectations, so much desire started floating in the mind of Shabnam. The next step was her admission to the college. Mumtaz wished to educate her loving daughter at any cost. 'Abbu' Shahjahan became enthusiastic to raise his daughter through proper education.

But *'Man proposes God disposes of.'* That's why a dark black chapter was about to commence in Shabnam's life.

6th Chapter

It was a calm morning. Shabnam getting up from bed was getting ready to set out to her school, where she would be felicitated by the school authority for her grand achievement in the examination. Mumtaz was busy with domestic duties. Shahjahan was getting ready to go out with his rickshaw. At that moment the *'Moulavi'* of the local mosque happened to arrive at the hut of Shahjahan. Shahjahan in helter-skelter receiving him made him sit inside the room. While chit-chatting Moulavi caused to pay heed to the messages of the Holy Quran to Shahjahan & Mumtaz. Finally, he raised the actual topic saying, *"Shahjahan, in our religious doctrine the more education of the women is not desirable. I came to know that your daughter Shabnam passed the school examination. Now no more education is permitted.Now think about her marriage."*Shahjahan said faltering,

"But Shabnam is desirous to prosper much in the life studying in college. Will it be proper to stop her admission in college studies now itself?"

"While following our religious doctrine you will have to do that. It's her befitting age for getting married. Everything will set-right once get married"

So long Mumtaz was listening to their conversation calmly. Now drawing the 'hijab' (veil) up to her face said humbly, *"Kindly excuse my insolence 'huzur'. My daughter's intrinsic nature for studies can hardly be ascertained. If we get her married giving up her admission to college, she won't be alive. I can perceive that considering our religious regulations we women should not be educated. But I heard that other Islamic countries allow their womenfolk to be educated. That's why I am afraid that if Shabnam gets married, her husband or her father-in-law's house may object to her education & stop her from going to college. By that not only Shabnam's dreams will be flittered away, but also her life will be foiled."*Telling at a stretch Mumtaz became out of breath.

Moulavi Saheb listening to Mumtaz with patience smilingly said, *'your word can't be ignored out of out. But I must tell you that a young man is very well known to me. He is educated & likes studies. He is in a good job in Mumbai with a fat salary per month.*

Such a brilliant boy shouldn't be out of hand. Shabnam can easily get admitted to college after getting married to this youth. More so there are ample facilities for education in Mumbai. Marrying that youth the dreams of Shabnam will be fulfilled as well as she can spend her happy & prosperous domestic life at Mumbai.'

'Whether that youth will agree to marry Shabnam, a girl of a penurious family like us?' Shahjahan became enthusiastic.

Moulavi Saheb said, *'That you leave to me. I have already talked to Siraj. Hereafter I will go to him & fix the date of marriage.'*

'Is it so? Is the name of the youth Siraj?' Mumtaz asked.

'Yes, Siraj. Sirajuddin Sheikh. An innocent boy. Dexterous & honest young man. He will be a good match with Shabnam.'

'Where is his dwelling-house? Who are his family members?' Shahjahan wanted to know.

'Originally they were residents of Murshidabad. But nowadays their dwelling place is in a village next to this village. I will bring this boy here. You will like that boy if you see him.'

Shabnam while returning from her school after being felicitated at school noticed that the *'Moulavi'* of a local mosque was coming out of her cottage. Shabnam observed hiding behind a tree that her 'Abbu' Shahjahan seeing off *'Moulavi'* with a smiling face.

Seeing off *Moulavi Saheb* Shahjahan entering the room said floating in jollity, *'Mumtaz, all these are due to 'doya' (Blessings) of **'Allah'**. Such good contact can't happen without the will of **'Allah'**.'*

Mumtaz listened to him calmly. But a black shadow was pricking in her heart.

As *'Moulavi Saheb'* left, Shabnam coming out from the hiding entering hut asked her 'Ammu' about the reason for the sudden & unexpected visit of *'Moulavi Saheb'* to their hut. Mumtaz frankly told her all the episodes.

That was a bolt from the blue on the head of Shabnam. *'Marriage! Then what will happen to her study in college?'* Tears were incessantly dropping down from the eyes of Shabnam. *'So her dreams of becoming successful in life will be nipped in the bud?'* Mumtaz tried to console her caressing her head. Coming near her Shahjahan tried to convince Shabnam saying, *'Shabnam don't be disheartened. This youth is well educated & likes education too. If you marry him your dream won't be frittered away. This youth after marriage returning to Mumbai will get you admitted to some good college. 'Moulavi Saheb' confirmed it.'* Listening to about the college at Mumbai Shabnam became somewhat pacified.

After a week *'Moulavi Shaheb'* arrived at the hut of Shabnam along with a youth named Siraj. Shahjahan with honor received them at the terrace of the hut & made them sit on the cot made by coir ropes. Mumtaz covering her face with a *'hijab'* carrying two plates containing some homemade sweets and cups of tea offered to the guests. While consuming the eatables *'Moulavi Saheb'* began the conversation about fixing the marriage.

In the meanwhile, Siraj expressed his desire to have a look at Shabnam. Shabnam so long was listening to their conversation hiding behind the wall. Mumtaz entering the room asked Shabnam to get ready to come out of the room. Covering the head with a gauze scarf Shabnam came out with her 'Ammu' and stood in front of the guests with a bashful look. Siraj looking at Shabnam smilingly asked, *'Shabnam I came to know from Moulavi Saheb that you want to get admitted to the college.'* Shabnam nodded her head bending her head bashfully. Siraj again repeated, *'You don't want to marry because of studying in college. Is it?'*

Shabnam keeping quiet didn't answer. Now Mumtaz

replied, *'Yes. She wants to get admitted to college. She is afraid that after marriage her husband or father-in-law's house may not like her to be educated. Hence her admission to the college will be obstructed. Thus her dreams of prosperity in life will become futile.'*

'Who told you that after marriage education will be stopped? Many married girls in Mumbai are working at different organizations after completion of their education. I can assure you that your daughter won't face any difficulty in her studies. There are so many renowned colleges in Mumbai. Shabnam will get admitted to any of the colleges. She can study as long as she desires.' Siraj assured Mumtaz.

'Now I have the reliance on your words. If that be the case, then my daughter may not remonstrate in marriage.' Mumtaz was assured by Siraj's' discourse.

Now *'Moulavi Saheb'* opened his mouth, *'Then let us settle the date of marriage. Mumtaz you can take away Shabnam now. Now we will discuss the fixation of marriage.'*

The wedding party was assembled in the courtyard of the local mosque pitching an awning. Because Siraj shouldered all the responsibilities of expenses for the wedding, penniless rickshaw puller Shahjahan heaved a sigh of relief. But those unaccountable expenses for the wedding by Siraj vacillated on account of doubt in the mind of Mumtaz but she had to keep mum considering their helplessness.

Putting on green *salwar*& *kameez* having an outfit designed with intricate *zari* embroidery Shabnam seemed to be a princess of some green island. Her head was covered by a greenish dupatta (Two folded sheets of cloth). One key piece of Gold jewelry known as *Jhoomar* was hanging attached to her left tuft of hair. Whatever pieces of jewelry required for a Muslim wedding were provided by Siraj for his bride Shabnam. Shabnam was embellished with a gold necklace, a pearl string, pair of thin gold bangles, small *ghungroos* on the anklet, a nose ring on the right side of her face, gold earring, and a gold finger-ring. Beautiful bridal *mehndi* designs were on the bride's hands & feet. Being dressed & decorated with bridal dressing Shabnam was sitting encircled by some rural Muslim womenfolk.

On the other side is dressed with the intricately embroidered golden *sherwani*& *churidaar* bridegroom was sitting encircled by some Muslim males. Only one gold neck chain and finger ring were his only ornaments. A costly wristwatch was on his right wrist and *Nagra* shoes on his feet.

Moulavi Saheb had officiated the Nikah or wedding ceremony. *Abbu* (Father) of Shabnam was appointed as *Wali* i.e. guardian to look after the bride Shabnam's interest in the *Nikah* by the *Moulavi Saheb*. Bridegroom Siraj's parents couldn't attend the wedding ceremony because of their illness. One of his distant relation the uncle being present presented *Mehr*(An amount of pre-decided cash) to seek bride Shabnam's consent for marrying the bridegroom Siraj. Next *Moulavi Saheb* began the *Nikah* praying from the holy **Quran**. He asked the bride Shabnam whether she was giving her consent to marry the bridegroom Siraj by accepting the *Mehr* uttering *'Qubool Hain'* thrice. Shabnam uttered the acceptance phrase *'Qubool Hai'* thrice. Then the *Moulavi Saheb* turning towards the bridegroom Siraj repeated the same phrase thrice. Groom Siraj repeated the same phrase thrice. That ritual is known as *'Liab-e-Qubool'*. Thereafter the bride Shabnam & groom Siraj had to sign the 'Nikahnama' i.e. wedding contract. Two witnesses each from the bride & groom's family signed as a witness. The *Nikahnama* outlines all possible duties and rites of both the bride and the groom as decreed by the **Quran**. Thereafter *Moulavi Saheb* recited paragraphs from the **Holy Quran** which are equivalent to marriage vows. Thereafter several rituals e.g. *Arsi Musharraf, Rukhsat, Walimah*, etc were conducted."

7th Chapter

So long narrating her life story at stretch Shabnam pauses for a while. It seems to me that she is seemed to be exhausted. I said, *"Shabnam, it appears from your face that you have become tired. Let us stop today. I will listen to your story some other day."*

Shabnam speaks out, *"No uncle I am not at all tired. My throat is dried. It will be all right after sipping water. I will narrate my entire story today. I don't know when we will meet again."*

"Then leave alone. Let me order two cups of tea."

As I ordered the waiter boy for two cups of tea, Shabnam getting up goes to a table having some glasses of water on it. Drinking water comes back to me. Meanwhile, the waiter brings two cups of tea. Shabnam & I start sipping tea. While drinking tea I ask Shabnam, *"Then you got married and went to Mumbai. Did Siraj get you admitted to the college at Mumbai?"*

As soon as I put the question, I have noticed Shabnam's eyes become moistened with tears. Being embarrassed I thought *'did I hurt Shabnam anyway?'* I express my feeling, *"Sorry Shabnam, did I hurt you by any means?"*

Without replying to me Shabnam bends her head down. Drops of tears are dripping down. The environment becomes grave. Keeping mum I have been staring at the face of Shabnam. I don't know how long we have been sitting like that. All of a sudden I have noticed that Shabnam getting up from her seat sprinkling water on her face comes & sits in front of me.

Just for lighting the topics, I say, *"Shabnam I have a wolf in my stomach. Let me order two plates of bread-butter & omelet. OK?"*

A slight smile is seen on the face of Shabnam now. Nodding her head she assents. I give an order for two plates. As two plates of bread butter & omelets are served, pushing a plate to Shabnam I say, "Shabnam eat so long it is hot. After consuming all we will go on chit-chatting."

Shabnam with a gloomy smile begins to make good use of the eatables keeping her head down. After eating while stirring the teacup unmindfully Shabnam, says, *'No uncle Siraj didn't get me admitted to any college at Mumbai. After the marriage ceremony, I accompanied by Siraj boarded on the train with a high hope & dream. At Mumbai, Siraj took me to a small room in the slum area. Being surprised when I asked Siraj about that small house, Siraj replied that getting good accommodation in Mumbai was very difficult. There were no provisions of cooking or any household goods. Siraj used to bring eatables from a nearby hotel. I stayed with him for one week as husband & wife. Though the 8' by 8' room was too small for a newly married couple, yet I adapted to that. Often Siraj used to tell that he would shift me to one of his anti, where I would be in a comfortable position."*

Keeping silent for a while Shabnam started narrating her

darkest days of life in Mumbai.

<u>8th Chapter</u>

"With intense longing for education as well as a profound dream for establishing in life within heart, newly married minor Shabnam boarded in the reserved compartment of Mumbai mail along with her husband Siraj. Abetting all the stresses of the train journey Shabnam became astonished entering a small room in a slum area of Mumbai. Shabnam noticed there was no separate kitchen or any utensils for cooking. Even there was no bathroom or latrine attached to the room. Stupefied Shabnam when asked about that 8' by 8'small room, Siraj replied sniggering *I am extremely sorry bringing you in this small room. It's very difficult to get good accommodation in the cultural society in Mumbai. However, I will try for better accommodation. Till such time I will keep you in the custody of my Mousi (Aunty). There you will be comfortable. Mousi will get you admitted to the college.'*

However, Shabnam adapted to that slum environment for about a week. Siraj used to bring lunch & dinner from the nearby hotel. Shabnam stayed in that small room for about a week with Siraj as a newly married couple.

'But what's about my admission to college?' Shabnam thought in anxiety. As she asked Siraj, he said, *'It's impossible to continue academic education in this environment of the slum area. That's why you will have to stay & study at my Mousi's house till I get proper accommodation. I will bear as much money is required for that. Don't worry about that.'*

Listening to that assurance from Siraj, Shabnam began weaving the net of the dream.

At dawn, the sunbeam was unable to penetrate the narrow slum area. There was no chirping of birds. The cooing of the cuckoo couldn't awaken the dweller of the confined slum area. Even then the sound of '*Azan*' from some distant mosque being floated in the air announced to be present in the prayer. Shabnam getting up from bed sat for '*Namaj*'. Siraj happened to go out to his working place. Shabnam didn't know the whereabouts of Siraj, where & which job he was attached to. Her credulous heart believed that certainly, Siraj was in a lofty job or a wealthy trader.

The morning advanced. A young married woman, dweller of the next door came & conversed with Shabnam. In the course of the conversation, Shabnam talked about her village life, about her schooling & sudden wedding with Siraj. Shabnam expressed her inclination in studies. The married woman told her name as Rukmini. Her husband Kumar Swami had a small food stall in the '*Nukkad*' *(Street corner)*. Their native place was the Madurai of Tamilnadu. She described the Minakshi Temple of Madurai. Shabnam listened to Rukmini's description of the gold-plated temple. Shabnam liked that soft-spoken Rukmini. Their intimacy grew further.

In an instant, one week passed by Shabnam in that confined environment. She became anxious about her admission to college, as promised by Siraj.

Shabnam thought of asking Siraj about that admission to college. While thinking so, Siraj entering the room in tempestuous speed asked Shabnam, '*Shabnam pack up your clothes & other necessary items and get ready. We will set out to my Mousi's house shortly. Keeping you there I will go out in search of good accommodation. Be ready now.*'
Shabnam enthusiastically arranging her own necessary

items asked Siraj, *'I am ready. Before leaving can I meet with my new friend Rukmini?'* As soon as Siraj nodding his head gave his consent, Shabnam set out to meet Rukmini.

Shabnam & Rukmini talked with each other about their weal & woe for a long. Meanwhile, Kumar Swami, the husband of Rukmini entered the room. Rukmini introduced Shabnam with Kumar Swami. As Kumar Swami heard that Shabnam would be shifted to the house of her husband's Mousi today, he gazing at Shabnam for a while said, *'Shabnamji are you acquainted with your husband's Mousi?'*

'No, I don't know her. My husband is searching for suitable accommodation for me. Till he gets the proper house, I will be with his Mousi.' Shabnam replied.

Kumar Swami being suspicious in mind said, *'Shabnamji always keeps it in mind that this is Mumbai City. Several peoples come here for various causes of demand. Your husband will shift you to Mousi's house. OK, but keep your eye & ear open. If you sense any adversity or feel any problem don't hesitate to contact us. I am giving you my phone number. You can get me all the time dialing me. Phone me telling everything unreservedly to me.'*

Kumar Swami writing his phone number on a piece of paper handing it over to Shabnam cautioned, *'Please don't divulge this phone no to your husband or anybody else. Keep it secret.'* Meanwhile, Siraj came & urged Shabnam to come out. Shabnam embracing Rukmini coming out of the room entered her room with Siraj.

Having lunch Siraj set out along with Shabnam. Shabnam followed Siraj with her small bag & baggage hiding the phone number in her purse.

Moving through the roundabout route, at last, the taxi entered into a thickly populated area. Siraj was sitting by the side of the taxi driver. Shabnam was affected by drowsiness sitting in the back seat of the taxi while dreaming of her admission to college. Entering the densely populated area as the taxi suddenly applied the brake, Shabnam woke up from drowsiness. She looked through the window & noticed the name of the road in an indistinct letter as Grant Road written in a shop. While passing through the road, there were several cinema halls Apsara, Jamuna, Minerva, Royal Talkies, Nishat Cinema so many more one after the other. She was delighted to see the well-congested area with so many picture halls, bakery shops, Temples, etc. far better than the slum area where she was taken by Siraj first.

As soon as the taxi started entering an area congested with huge numbers of hotels & lodges, Shabnam tried to locate the name of the place & found a name written on a hotel at Kamathipura. Some two-three low-grade movie theatres are also found. There were so many narrow lanes. A lot of crowds were found to be gathered around the lanes. So many girls wearing colorful dresses & passionate cosmetics were found standing on the corner of the lanes. Shabnam was amazingly thinking *what the shameless girls standing on the street!'* She turned her eyes from them. Meanwhile, the taxi stopped near a lane marked as the 6th lane. Siraj got down with Shabnam. The taxi driver looked at Shabnam with a mysterious smile before moving the taxi. Siraj told Shabnam that they had arrived at the house of his 'Mousi'

A telephone booth was found at the entrance of the lane. While following Sirajuddin, Shabnam took out the piece of paper from her purse & secretly mugged up the phone number of Kumar Swami. She thought, *'if by chance the paper is misplaced, better to keep it in memory.'* She kept the paper in her purse.

Walking a furlong away Siraj stopped in front of an old 'Haveli', named as Shakila Manjil'. It was a two-storied building. Pushing a large wooden door Sirajuddin entered in with Shabnam. Before asking anything Siraj said, *'Shabnam, this is my Mousi's haveli.'*

'Such a large haveli! Who is Shakila? Siraj's Mousi?' Shabnam was observing the nooks & corners of the house with eyes widened with amazement.

A very big courtyard was in front, at the corner of which was a scaffold of sacred basil. A girl was found pouring water on the holy basil & bowed with folded hands. *'How is it?'* Shabnam thought, *'this manzil belongs to some Muslim woman Shakila. Why then basil scaffold is here?'* In her village, Shabnam saw several Holy Basil scaffolds in the houses of Hindu villagers. Before she put this question to Siraj, a buxom old Muslim woman chewing betel leaf coming out of a room said in a harsh voice, *'heigh Sirajuddin! You've brought my Beti (daughter). Welcome, welcome. Come in with her.'* Shabnam observed that sweet-tongued woman, wearing green *'salwar, kamij '*, a black *'hijab'* on her head, leaps dyed with chewing betel leaf, a costly golden framed spectacle on eyes. Now the shadow of doubt was removed from Shabnam. *'Yes, Mousi is Muslim. But why holy basil scaffold then?'* Mousi turning back noticing Shabnam looking at the scaffold said, *'several Hindu girls stay here as a tenant. That's why that scaffold of Basil leaf.'* Being embarrassed Shabnam hurriedly said, *'No Mousi, I haven't thought that way. There are several holy basil scaffolds in our village. That's why I was looking at that.'* Mousi chuckled & said, *'Are you nostalgic about your village? Don't worry you will forget that while staying here in town. Come on sit on the chair. It seems you have a dry tongue.'* Staring at Siraj Mousi snubbed, *'You haven't fed my 'beti' properly.'* Saying so Mousi loudly called some working girl, *'Farida, bring two glasses of 'Sarbat' & sweets for my beti & Siraj'*. After a while, the girl named Farida brought two glasses of *'Sarbat'* & sweet in a plate & gave to Shabnam & Siraj.

While drinking *'sharbat'* Siraj said, *'Mousi I am keeping my 'bibi' Shabnam under your custody for a few days. I am in search of a good rented house. I will take her away once I get the house.'* Mousi said giggling, *'Why for few days? What's the harm if my sweet beti is kept here with me?'*

'No Mousi' Siraj said anxiously, *'She wants to get admitted to a college. That's why I am thinking of taking her away.'*

'Oh! For this reason? Then what's the use of taking her away with you? She will be here with peace & happiness. Admission to college? That I can also arrange for that.'

'Ok Mousi, then get her admitted to your college. I will come later on & take her away with me. For the time being let her be here.' Saying so, Siraj giving some money to Shabnam said *'Shabnam during admission to the college you will require some money. Keep this amount with you. Mousi will arrange everything for your admission to college. Don't worry. I will come occasionally to get information about you. Now let me push off.'*

Initially, Shabnam was spending a few days comfortably under the affection & fondling of Mousi. Shabnam was allotted a well-furnished single room. A working maid was kept to take care of her & to run errands. The name of the maid was Shabana, a shy & sweet girl. Shabnam was fascinated by the cordiality of Mousi. But after few days Shabnam was disillusioned. During the evening Shabnam was not allowed to go out of the room. She used to play ludo with Shabana. Occasionally Mousi used to come in the room caressing Shabnam on her head. So one day when Mousi entered the room, Shabnam asked Mousi about her admission to college. Mousi smilingly said, '*Oh yes. I remember that my beti. I will take you tomorrow to a professor at the college. He will arrange everything for your admission to college.*' As soon as Mousi left the room Shabnam embraced Shabana being delighted for her admission to college. Shabana after being released from Shabnam was looking at her with tearful eyes. For the last few days, Shabana became compassionate about Shabnam. That's why in a gushing stream of tears Shabana embraced Shabnam. Keeping her head on Shabnam's chest she was going on shedding tears. Then, all of a sudden she left the room running while shedding tears. Being astonished Shabnam following her came out of the room. And then only a scene came to her notice in the wide hall from behind a pillar.

In front of Mousi so many girls with impudent dressings were standing in rows. Some strong & stubborn fellows were standing near the wall. Some well-dressed persons coming one after the other, depositing some money in the hand of Mousi, were taking away their selected girls to the scheduled rooms.

The picture became crystal clear in the mind of Shabnam. Shabnam could perceive that she had been trapped in the clutch of a brothel. Siraj sold her to Mousi of the brothel house. '*How to flee from this den of hell?*' Shabnam became anxious about her future.

Shabnam thought whether Mousi would really take her to a professor. Else she would have any scheme of selling Shabnam to any other person. She was unable to sleep being solicitous. She was tossing about on the bed. All of a sudden getting up she started sobbing covering her face with palms, feeling about her helplessness.

Shabana was in deep sleep on a bed on the floor by the side of Shabnam's cot. Listening to the sobbing of Shabnam, she woke up. Getting up she sat by the side of Shabnam, embracing her tried to console her. Now, Shabnam began expressing all her anecdotes starting from schooling to marriage with Sirajuddin. Listening to those anecdotes of Shabnam, Shabana also began her heartrending life story. Orphan Shabana was brought to Bombay from Bangladesh by her maternal uncle & sold to this brothel.

Since then helpless Shabana was compelled to stay here under the custody of Mousi, working as a maidservant. Off & on she was compelled to share the bed with different unknown clients. In this way, she had to spend about two years with suppressed hatred within the heart.

While listening to her piteous episode, Shabnam asked in a low voice, *'Is there any way to escape from this place?'* Listening to her query startled Shabana hastily went near the door, cautiously opening it looking outside this way & that, very carefully shut the door. Coming near Shabnam she said in low voice, *"Shabnam Didi, here wall has also got an ear. Hence be careful."* Being disappointed Shabnam said heaving a deep sigh, *'So, there is no way to get rid of this hellish life?'*

'How to get out of this hell? Some invisible eyes always are keeping an eye, especially on those who have come here recently.'

'You are not new to this brothel Shabana. Can't you go out of this house?'

'Yes, Mousi knows very well that I don't have any place to escape. That's why I am permitted to go to the market or shop off & on.'

Listening to this Shabnam recalled the name of Kumar

Swami & Rukmini. The phone number of Kumar Swami written on a piece of paper is still safely kept in the purse of Shabnam.

Shabnam very cautiously taking out the paper from her purse, writing the phone number & name of Kumar Swami on a piece of paper, kept the paper containing the phone number of Kumar Swami in her purse. Coming near Shabana Shabnam asked in a low voice, *'Shabana can you help me a bit?'*

'Help? Tell me what am I to do.'

'OK, I will tell. Before that, you tell me when will you go to the market?'

'Market? Yes, tomorrow I will have to go to the market to purchase some fruits for Mousi.'

'Then listen to. Very carefully you have to do this job. Can you do it?'

'You just tell & see whether I can do it or not.'

'Can you give a phone call to one of my relatives, residing in Mumbai? You will have to perform the job very cautiously. If you are caught then both of us will be submerged in the darkness.'

'What darkness! We are staying in darkness only. Just to get out of this darkness, I will have to try. Now you tell whom to be phoned & what to tell?'

'You phone up to one Kumar Swami and tell, 'Shabnam is in danger. She has been sold by her husband at Shakila Manjil, on the 6th lane of Grant road. Please rescue Shabnam.''

Shabnam handed over the paper containing the name & phone number of Kumar Swami to Shabana. Shabana kept the paper hidden in the inner pocket of her 'kamij'.

Now both of them lay down on bed being relieved from anxiety. It was midnight. Slumber descended down on the eyes of Shabnam."

<u>9th Chapter</u>

Saying up to this covering her face with her arms Shabnam sits with her head down. A deep sigh comes out of her heart. I didn't want to embarrass her by asking questions further. Keeping silent for some time, summoning the waiter of the restaurant I ordered two cups of tea. The boy cleverly brings two pieces of cake along with two cups of tea. I look attentively at Shabnam. I could feel her woeful tale of the past is scratching her heart. After a while removing her arm from her eyes, observing the cakes & tea, Shabnam speaks hurriedly, *"What's the matter uncle! You have ordered for tea again?"*

"Yes, I ordered it. Your throat might have dried out while narrating your anecdotes so long. Quickly moisten your throat. You will sound well." Without replying to anything she picks up the cup & starts sipping. As I pushed the plate of cake, she says, *"Oh! You have brought the cake too!"*

I cut the joke, *"Narrating such a long story your stomach might have become empty. Come on eat the cake. You will feel energized."* Shabnam now snorts & says, *"Uncle, Will you not listen to my subsequent stories of struggle?"* Observing that she has become somewhat normal I say, *"Oh yes. I must listen to it. What happened after that? What's the name of the girl you told?"*

"Shabana, Shabana is her name?"

"Oh yes. Shabana, Shabana. Could she phone up to the person's phone no, you gave it to her?"

"Uncle Mousi used to keep some watcher behind every one of us.

Whenever Shabana used to go out for marketing a watcher was behind her also. Shabana could sense that a watcher was following her. Treating no importance to it she entered a fruit shop. While purchasing the fruits she requested the shopkeeper to hold the purchased fruits for a while till she would come back from the urinal. She could observe that the watcher was keeping eyes on her movement from a distance. Shabana entered the urinal for ladies & shut the door behind. Coming out of the urinal through the back door she went to a nearby telephone booth and phoned Kumar Swami. Informing all the episodes about Mousi, she told him in short 'please save Shabnam'. Entering the urinals again, washing hands, came out of the urinals through the front door wiping her hand. She observed that the watcher was standing at the same place at a distance. Without looking at him, picking up the fruits bag from the shopkeeper Shabana set out towards 'haveli'."

Listening to the episode I hurriedly say, *"Bravo! Cunningly she phoned Kumar Swami. The watcher couldn't suspect anything. Then what happened?"*

"Shabana entering the 'haveli' straightway coming to Mousi handed over the fruits bag to her. Settling up the account to Mousi, Entering my room she shut the door. Handing over the paper of phone number to me, said in low voice, 'Shabnam, Kaam ho gaya.'. That's it. I was sure that Kumar Swami would take proper action. Telling Shabana to keep mum asked her to wait for the action."

Thereafter the heart-rending story of Shabnam is being uttered unobstructed & rapidly.

<u>10th Chapter</u>

"Shabnam & Shabana while waiting for the freedom from

this hellish suffering became drowsy. *'It is about evening, there is no hint of freedom! In that case did Kumar swami not informed properly? Else he got the information but couldn't do anything?'* While thinking so, the eyes of Shabnam became closed.

On the other side, the evening started descending. In the large hall of *'Haveli'* trafficking of girls began in front of Mousi. Frequenting of the clients started. Shabana was observing that from hiding. At such a time an informer entering the *'Haveli'* panting shouted, *'Mousi, police, police van has come. There may be a police raid here.'*

Listening to him Mousi ordered all the rowdies to hide all the girls in the dungeon, Shabana swiftly ran away & entering the room of Shabnam excitedly said, *'Shabnam get up*. Police have come.' Shabnam springing up smartly said being excited, *'Police! Where?* Have *they come here?'* Before she finished her words, two rowdies entering the room holding the hands of both dragging them pushed in a semi-dark room while tying their arms & feet, sticking adhesive tape on their mouth came out of the room & shut the door.

How long both Shabnam & Shabana were lying captive not known to them. After some time they listened to the sound of a heavy boot. Shabnam tried to scream but only groaning came out from her adhesive-taped mouth. Helpless Shabnam started weeping. She heard the voice of Mousi, saying, *'Sir this room is full of old discarded furniture & refuse matters. If you want I can open & show to you sir that nobody stays here.'* A gravely male voice of policeman was heard, *'That's all right. You need not open this. Show other rooms too.'*

Listening to their sound of departure, Shabnam & Shabana somehow went rolling near the door, started striking the door forcefully with their legs. As the police team was about to depart, Kumar Swami & other members of the NGO abruptly stopped. *'Aren't some sound coming out from that closed room!'* Kumar swami came forward near the room, opening the bolt of the room wide open the door. He found that two girls were lying on the floor with their hands, legs & mouth in tied condition. Kumar swami & others put their hands to untie them & brought them out in the light. The police office sarcastically asked Mousi, *'Are these two girls your old furniture?'* Mousi stood with her head down. Kumar Swami holding the hand of Shabnam said to the police officer, *'Sir, She is Shabnam. She was sold by her husband Sirajuddin to this brothel.'*

That day police handed over ten girls & Shabana in the custody of the voluntary organization. Shabnam wanted to keep Shabana with her but the police objected. Police arrested Mousi and her six associates & locked them in the prison of the police station. Police sealed the *'haveli'*. Of course, Mousi was released from police custody after signing a bond that hereafter she won't trade the abducted girls in the future. Kumar swami took Shabnam in his own custody to his house. Mumbai police contacted West Bengal police about Shabnam. After few days police force from West Bengal arrived at Mumbai police station along with

Shabnam's father, Shahjahan. Mumbai police took them to the house of Kumar Swami. Shahjahan expressed gratitude to Kumar Swami for taking care of his daughter. Shabnam took leave of Rukmini suffused with tears. Rukmini embraced Shabnam weeping incessantly. Shabnam touching the feet of Kumar Swami before departure said, *'Dada I would have rotted in the hell if you wouldn't be there. I can't forget your beneficence throughout my life. If I could get on in life, I will again come & meet with you & Rukmini.'*

Shabnam set out with West Bengal police & Shahjahan.

Arriving at Shabnam's home in the village of Nadia district, Mumtaz coming out of the room embraced Shabnam, her dearest daughter. Both of them started shedding tears. Police were observing their scene of reunion. At the end of their wailing moment of reunion, the police officer while listening to all the episodes of Shabnam's marriage recorded in his diary, sitting in front of both of them. The *'Maulavi'*, who proposed the matrimonial alliance for Shabnam was taken under police custody. Cross-examining the *'Maulavi'* police could find the trace of the artificial uncle of Sirajuddin. Uncle Muhammad Alam was arrested from his house in the village of Burdwan. On cross-examination, police came to know that both the *'Maulavi'* & uncle were involved in the conspiracy gang of women abduction. *But where is the main culprit Sirajuddin?* As per the description of Shiraj by Shabnam, a portrait was drawn by a police artist. The copies of that portrait were sent to different police stations of different districts. A combing operation was going on everywhere.

At last, information received from a police station of Murshidabad that a wedding was going to be conducted between a bride Shayama Ghatak with a youth Rabin Goswami, a dweller of Mumbai. The parent of Shayma was a very indigent family. That's why getting an alliance of well-to-do youth, they didn't want to delay. They agreed to the marriage.

Police got information that Robin Goswami was

shouldering the entire expanses of the wedding. Police suspicion became a firm belief. The police officer of Nadia district was informed. The police officer set out for Murshidabad along with Shabnam & her parent.

The wedding ceremony was in the village Bahadurpur of Murshidabad. Tiny bulbs of different colours were burning in the well-decorated venue of the wedding ceremony. The tune of the flute was being played in low voice. The sound *'ulu'* by the local women was being heard off & on. The venue of the wedding was being sonorous by the invitees.

When the wedding party was brightening up bantering with the bride & bridegroom, a police vehicle arrived at the outside of the pavilion indiscernibly. The police officer of the local police station came out along with the police officer of Nadia & six-armed polices.

With the presence of police in the wedding pavilion, everyone became flabbergasted. The Father of the bride came running to the police officers in a nervous hurry. Folding his arms he said, *'Sir, my daughter has crossed the age of 18 years. I can show you her birth certificate. That's why I have arranged a marriage for her. I haven't done anything wrong. Then who has informed you wrongly sir?'*

'Yes, we got the same information that the bride is below 18 years. That's why we have come. Now we find you are correct. Then there is no way to prevent the wedding. OK let it go' the Local Police officer said concealing their actual motive of coming there.

The police officer of Nadia now asked the father of the bride, *'Bravo! It looks very nice your daughter's wedding party. You have decorated the pavilion in pomp & grandeur. You have spent a lot of money on this. Is it not?'*

'Thank you, sir. All the expenditures of my daughter's wedding have

been shouldered by my bridegroom Robin. He is a nice guy. He is a wealthy person having a business in Mumbai. He will take care of my daughter well.'

'Very nice! Can we have a look at your bridegroom?' The police officer said.

'Oh yes. Please come with me. I will get him acquainted with you all.' The police team entered the wedding pavilion following the father of the bride. The bridegroom was wearing costly linen *'Panjabi'* & *'Dhoti'.* Wearing *'topor'* (a traditional coronet) on the head he was sitting with a tranquil smile on the face. Staring at the police in the pavilion, Robin became perplexed. A police officer of the local police station said while smiling, *'Mr. Robin we have come here to converse & greet you. We are from the local police station. Don't worry about that. We came to know from the father of the bride that you are bearing the entire expanses of the marriage. Oh, it's very good. We heard that you have a business in Mumbai. If you don't have any inconvenience please tell us about your business.'*

All of a sudden the face of the bridegroom became pale. Somehow retraining he falteringly said, *'No it's not a big one. Some light & paltry business of clothing.'*

So long the police super of Nadia was going on listening to their discourse. Now without wasting time, he charged Robin directly, *'Robin your business & activities are in the Grant Street of Mumbai. Is it not?'* Listening to the word 'Grant Street' the bridegroom's face became abashed once more. He immediately refuted, *'No, No Sir. Why grant street? My working places are at Dadar, Navi Mumbai.'*

'Oh! Is it? So dear child tell me what is your real name? Is it Robin or, Sirajuddin or Muhammad Selim or Kabir Ray so on & so forth? By which name I should call you?'

'What are you talking Sir? By no means, I do have these names. My

name is Robin. Robin Chakravarty.'

'Chakravarty! But we came to know your name is Robin Goswami. How is it?'

Now the father of the bride opened his mouth, *'what are you saying, sir? My son-in-law's name is Robin Goswami Sir.'*

'Yes, we came to know that only. But your would-be son-in-law is telling his name is Robin Chakravarty. Is it not?'

'He might have wrongly uttered that. Since you are asking several questions to him; that's why he told in a slip of tongue being afraid.'

'That may be. But you didn't tell your name so far.'

'I am Ramjivan Ghatak.'

'Ramjivan Babu, who has brought this alliance for your daughter?'

'She is Dulari Devi, resident of this locality. She brought alliances of several girls of this locality. She is a trustworthy well-behaved person. She is here in the pavilion. Shall I call her?'

'Noh, don't call her now. Ramjivan Babu, you better postpone this marriage now. Are you giving your daughter to an undeserving miscreant?'

'Just wait. It will be clear to you shortly.' The local police officer said.

Police Super of Nadia district gesticulated to the police to bring Shabnam.

Shabnam along with her parent arrived at the spot. Police super showing the bridegroom standing with hanging down his head asked Shabnam, *'Shabnam just look at this person. Can you recognize this man?'*

Before Shabnam saying anything, Mumtaz shouted, *'Sir this is that man Sirajuddin, who cheated my daughter.'*

Shabnam now coming forward standing front to front giving a powerful slap on the face of that miscreant said, *'Sir, this is Sirajuddin, who marrying me sold in a brothel of Grant Street of Mumbai. This rascal must be punished severely so that he won't get any opportunity to ruin any girl utterly.'* Shabnam closing her face started sobbing.

Police Super seizing by neck dragging Robin alias Sirajuddin snubbed, *'you rascal, how long you are in this trading? How many girls you have abducted?'*
Robin alias Sirajuddin sitting down embracing the leg of Police Super screamed, *'Sir I made a blunder. Kindly pardon me, sir. I will never do this kind of mischief.'*
Pulling him with a sudden forceful jerk giving a heavy slap ordered police to handcuff Siraj & take him to the police van.

Now Mritunjay Sanyal alias Muhammad Ilius, the fake maternal uncle of Siraj was arrested. Observing that arrest Dulari Devi tried to escape from the spot but caught red-handed by police.

Then the local police officer said to the father of the bride, *'Ramjivan Babu, your daughter is narrowly escaped. If she would have got married to that fraud person, he would have sold your daughter to any brothel. It's your good luck that we arrived at the correct moment & rescued your daughter. Now you arrange your daughter's marriage with some local boy. We will help you in this regard.'*

The father of the bride stood like a log being spellbound due to that sudden occurrence. Police Van set out with the arrested culprits."

11th Chapter

Drawing rein to the past story, Shabnam says, *"Uncle, I arrived at the last period of those days of a nightmare."*
"That fake maternal uncle of Sirajuddin Muhammad Ilius

& Dulari Devi was arrested by police. Any more culprits were arrested by police force?"

"Yes, uncle. After thorough investigation & hunting up & down, police forces could arrest entire gangs of abductors of women from different parts of West Bengal, e.g. Canning, Diamond harbor, Harrows, Basirhat area. Besides that, some schemers were located in the neighboring states like Bihar & Orissa and Nepal. They were also taken in custody of the police."

"Oh! Then a large gang of abductors was captured! I presume that after these rings of conspirators were arrested the abduction was stopped."

"Yes, momentarily it was stopped. But gradually some new gangs were originated."

"Of course that is a continuous process. It's the duty of the police to investigate & collectively arrest these culprits. However, what happened to you after that incident?"

"Uncle, I returned to our village along with my parents. But in the eyes of our neighbor, it seemed I was guilty. Hence we decided to depart from the village."

"Well. After the wedding of you with Siraj, did your mother leave the job of the nursery school?"

"After returning from Mumbai to the village, I came to know that my Ammu desired to resign from the nursery school. But as requested by the authority of the nursery school, she had to continue in the job. In the meanwhile, my Abbu discontinued driving the rickshaw & started driving a van in the town. That's why when we decided to leave the village, my ammu arranged a rented house on the outskirts of the township. Hence, once at dawn, we left the village secretly towards the township loading all the household articles on the van. And an afresh struggle of life began in my life."

"Struggle of life!" I look at her face in astonishment.

"Yes, uncle. A struggle for existence. My stream of life never flew in

an easily accomplished manner. At every moment colliding against different rocks, flowing through various obstructions I had to proceed further."

"That obstruction was ended after your wedding turmoil."

"No uncle. Nothing came to the end after my wedding turmoil. It was not like that."

"Then? What else other reasons?"

"Uncle I took birth in an extremely indigent family. Not only indigence, but my birth was also in a family of an illiterate Muslim parent. My birth was in such a Muslim society, where female offspring is considered as unwanted matter, where leave aside the education of the female child, the ruling was issued to spend the life behind the black curtain at the nook of the house. Nobody dared to disregard that ruling of mollas or maulavis, on the other hand, common Muslims used to believe that ruling was Allah's ruling."

"Even then you could study from childhood."

"Yes. That I could. In that, there was assent from my ammu & abbu secretly. Especially the acceptance of the job by my ammu as a caretaker in the nursery school at township was most helpful for my study. But that matter about my study in the nursery was kept secret from the Muslim society of the village."

"But your study in the high school in your village certainly couldn't be kept a secret?"

"Uncle, the high school in our village had been far away from the Muslim-dominated area near the border of the suburb area. There also had to face extreme hostilities during my admission since I was the daughter of a Muslim. But observing my incredible obstinacy for getting admission to the school some of the school's female teachers put some educative questions to me. Being satisfied with my correct reply they recommended for my admission."

"After getting admitted I hope you could continue your studies effortlessly?"

"Yes, that should have been. But no, my studies didn't progress effortlessly. Since I am being a daughter of an illiterate Muslim rickshaw puller, I continued my studies sitting on the backbench as an untouchable student. But observing my excessive zeal & attention in studies the female teacher arranged for me to sit on the first bench. Though, other girl students used to evade my touch. Thereafter came the days of examination. I stood in the first position securing the highest marks in all the papers. Thereafter I was going on topping the list in the entire class examinations one after the other in an irresistible way. Finally, I passed the higher secondary examination in the first division with letter marks in all the subjects & occupied the first position within the district level. That period was the golden era of my life.

But after that, the hindrances began against my lifestream."

"Hindrance! Why? What happened to you?"

"Uncle the news of my success reached the Maulavi of the mosque of the village. Consequent to that the seeds of the poison trees were implanted in the soil of the mosque. And that seed grew as a plant bringing an alliance for my marriage. The consequent episode I have already told to you."

"Yes, I listened to your event of atrocious days. But what happened to your admission to college after shifting your house to the town? I presume certainly you didn't face any more disturbances."

"Uncle did I not tell you that disturbances are indissolubly linked to my life."

"Why? Did you face any more problems there?"

"It was my all along desire to get admitted to some girls' college of Kolkata. And for that, I tried to get some accommodation in a rented small house in Kolkata. I got some houses too in some cultured society. But my name is Shabnam Mondal. My religion is Islam. Consequently, all the owners of the houses refused to let out for rent to a Muslim girl. Stumbling at various places, at last, I got

accommodation in a mess for women at a Muslim inhabited place at Park Circus. It was astonishing that not only Muslim girls but also some Hindu & Christian girls in that mess became my companions. Muhammad Jakir Hosen, the owner of that mess was a well-educated, affectionate & modest person."

"Very good. Then it was an excellent one. Being stumbled at various places, at last, you got a modest accommodation to live long happily."

"Yes, that I got. But you know that my ammu & abbu didn't have any means to support the expenditures of my college studies & house rents."

"What did you do then? Did you start tutoring the school students to maintain the expenditures?"

"No uncle. Of course, initially, I thought to earn by tutoring the school students. But that was also conditional on time. Then I thought of disposing of the inauspicious ornaments which I received during my marriage. That's why once I sold all the ornaments & the money received I kept it in my newly opened account in a bank. That enormous amount of money I got by selling the ornaments utilized for my studies.

But obstruction came during the admission in girls' college. The principal of the college listening to my episode of marriage & selling to the brothel at Mumbai from me, objected to my admission to keep other girl students away from the proximity of mine. My persistent request, supplication all became futile. Being disappointed I returned to mess while sobbing.

Observing me sitting with tearful eyes house owner Jakir Sahib asked me, 'Beta what happened to you why are you sitting with a sad face?' Wiping my eyes I narrated my entire episodes of life as well as what happened in the college to him. Listening to me he kept quiet for a while & said, 'Tomorrow you come with me to the college.'

The next day Jakir Sahib along with me entered the

chamber of the principal of the college. Noticing Jakir Sahib in her chamber Mrs. Chakravorty, the principal of the college, cordially received him getting up from the chair. She offered him to take the chair. Standing at the corner of the room, I could perceive that Jakir Sahib was not only very much acquainted with her but also Jakir Sahib was in very much venerable person.

Now raising my life history top to bottom asked her, 'Madam, now you tell, in these course of events where is the guilt of this girl? She became a victim of the circumstances. She could come out from that pit of hell having recourse to a contrivance and not only that with the help of police forces she could entrap the women abductor gangs & arrest them extensively. This girl occupied the first position in Higher Secondary Examination within the Nadia district. Her only meditation & cognition is to flourish in life educating her. If you don't cooperate with her sympathetically then her vision will become futile. She is a tenant of my mess. Considering her financial constraint I offered her rent-free accommodation. But her perception of self-esteem she refused to accept that free offer with humble submission & agreed to stay in the mess at a small house rent. Now you tell can you not assist this girl about her education & admission in your college?'

So long after listening to the entire episode of my life, Mrs. Chakravarty agreed to get me admitted to the college. Thanking a lot to Mrs. Chakravarty, Jakir Sahib returned home along with me."
"So nice. You got admitted to girls' college. Luckily Jakir Sahib came forward for your help. Thereafter I hope you didn't face any more problems in college?"
Shabnam with a gloomy smile says, "Uncle, the problem became my life companion. I got admitted in the first year with arts in the college. I lost one year because of my fake marriage, abduction to Mumbai, hide & seek between the police & the women abductor gang, extensive arrests by police. Even then that admission in the college

*was a boon of **Allah**.*

On the first day, I entered the classroom along with the students with palpitation in the heart. I noticed all the girl students were evading me. I got a seat at the corner of the last bench. I remembered my school days. Initially being a daughter of a Muslim rickshaw puller I had to sit on the last bench. Of course, afterward occupying the first position in the examination, I was permitted to sit on the first bench. In this college to this didn't become otherwise. My apparel, the impression of penury on my face was dissimilar with the daughters of the wealthy of peoples of our class. Consequently, I was considered an outcast in the eyes of those girls. My self-esteem interdicted me to consider anything other than studies. Now I solemnly resolved I won't take a seat on the first bench even I secure a good position in the examinations.

Hence digesting & keeping quiet the entire leering glance, disregards of my fellow students I deeply concentrated on my studies. Here also occupying the first potion in the entire examinations one after the other I passed the fourth year final examination in first class with honors in social science.

During that college period Principal Mrs. Chakravarty madam, several times asked me to take a seat on the first bench. I thanked her humbly replied, 'Madam, there is no difference between first or last bench to me. The main thing is the concentration of mind.'

After completion of the college chapter now I am a student at Kolkata University. But still, I stay at the Park Circus area under the affectionate care of Jakir Sahib. That magnanimous person accepting house rent from me is a far cry; he gives all the financial help to me for my studies.

Uncle if you happened to come to Park Circus on any day, please come to my rented house. I will introduce you to that magnanimous good-hearted Jakir Sahib.

The evening is descending down. If I return home late at night my fatherly guardian will rebuke me."

I was listening to Shabnam's biography so long being spellbound. I am not willing to leave her to depart now itself. Even then she will have to return.

I say, "Do you go to your ammu & abbu?"

"Yes, uncle of course I go. They are the origin of my life. Every Sunday visiting them I get peace of mind. I have come from them only today. Now let me push off."

All of a sudden Shabnam bowed down to touch my feet & set out.

I stare at my yellow butterfly's path of departure. I pray to God for her endeavor to be successful in life.

<u>Last Chapter</u>

Thereafter my hackneyed life stream flows through various variegation. Days after days, months after months were spent in the opera festival in the theatrical stage of seasons. My pen didn't be at rest in the parlor of nature. Off & on looking at nature I contemplate that where the six seasons are which I saw, I perceived during my childhood? Where have you lost the invocatory of Summer, Rainy, Autumn, Dewy, Winter, Spring seasons? As if the atmosphere of the world has started changing gradually. In India due to the flogging of the heatwave of acrid summer drought is declared at many places. The shower of fire of scorching Sun scalded & dried the crops of the land. The wailing of the cultivators spread in heaven & earth. Also, we observe due to heavy shower virulence of deluge in many states. We come to know that in the mountain region due to keen rainfall the hilly roads are being collapsed by the landslide. The torrents of the mountainous rivers demolishing the shore are drifting away from the inhabited places. What a devastating game of nature! Again we observe at the advent of transitory winter many regions are very much stricken with severe cold waves. In the mountainous region the mercury while declining more & more arrives at below zero degrees. Hence now there are no six seasons but only three seasons. The fury of the three seasons creates bewilderment with fright in the mind of human beings.

Within this capriciousness of season trio, my pen started moving composing various novels one after the other. While weaving the snare of imaginary portraits how many years passed I couldn't pay heed to it.

I came back to my senses when all of a sudden an invitation came from my publisher of Chennai to attain the world book fair at Pragati Maidan of New Delhi, where my novel published internationally would be displayed. I startled! Delhi! That also in the month of January, in between cold waves! Besides that, I was getting news on social media about the extremely polluted atmosphere in Delhi. I was wavering for going to Delhi. After a few days a phone call came from the publisher, *'Are you coming? A hotel is already booked for you.'*
Now I couldn't have a difference of opinion. Giving consent I purchased two Railway tickets in Rajdhani Express.

On the scheduled time & date the Rajdhani Express arrived at New Delhi. I & my wife came down from the compartment on the platform. While coming on my way to Delhi I noticed a heavy shower outside of the compartment. Now coming out of the platform I noticed a cloudless clear atmosphere. Where had dispersed the dusty atmosphere of New Delhi! Where the pollution disappeared, which veiled the sky of Delhi? I inhaled fully in a clean atmosphere. I thanked nature for presenting a cloudless; dust-free clean Delhi by strong blow of shower washing all the pollution from the atmosphere. Before traveling to Delhi I came to know that the temperature of Delhi was near 3-4 degrees Celsius. That's why we carried huge woolen garments. But what is it! Due to a heavy shower at night the temperature of Delhi was ascending.

We arrived at the hotel FAB carrying our heap of warm clothing. Well decorated, spick & span hotel. Entering the already booked room removing the woolen coat, sweeter, throwing on a sofa, both of us lounged on the brilliantly white & clean bed.

World Book Fair. In front of a large poster of the World Book Fair, I snapped many photographs of my wife. We went around various stalls of the fair. Countless publishers were displaying their variegated published books on so many beautiful racks. We were becoming enchanted while visiting displays of various stalls. My publisher got me acquainted with their other writers & snapping our combined photographs spread on social media for publicity. I introduced my wife to a writer & his wife. Their son snapped our combined photograph. When we were engaged in chit-chatting, all of a sudden a message came on my WhatsApp from my granddaughter demanding two novels written by some renowned English novelists. We took leave from my writer's family and set out in search of those two invaluable novels, one of the two being Austen Jane. We whirl around several bookstalls of several halls. But in vain. While coming out of a hall, I noticed some large posters of the NBT list of books in Hindi & English. As advertised by NBT we entered hall no.11 consists of approx 173 stalls displaying variegated books on several racks. Searching nooks & corners of the stalls for the novels I couldn't locate the same novels. While whirling around I became exhausted. Suddenly I noticed a stall of Penguin publisher. I felt that presumably, those two novels might be available in that Penguin stall. There was a large crowd in the Penguin stall. Penguin is a renowned publisher. Here most of the English books/novels written by world-famous novelists. I noticed enormous numbers of crowds were entering within the stall; especially the book-lovers were mostly students of school & colleges. Their deportments & dresses seemed to me that they might have belonged to a highly educated & wealthy community. A person like me, an old person was inappropriate in the stream of those elite communities. I had no other go. I had to enter the stall in search of the novels demanded by my granddaughter. The racks were embellished with various variegated books. I started groping the racks after racks. Finally, I could pick up the desired two novels and stand in a queue for paying the price of the novels.

Paying the amount somehow I came out of the stall gasping for breath. At that moment I noticed a female youth came out of the stall with some books in hand forcing through the crowd saying in Bengali dialect while gasping, *"Oh what a crowd! I heave a sigh of relief."*
Listening to the Bengali dialogue from her I looked at her in surprise & found she was a smart adult girl. She was having a dull complexion, wearing a sunglass, green 'Salwar

& Kamij', a costly wristwatch on her left wrist, and a thin gold chain on her neck. She didn't have any more embellishments. But her countenance was dignified. Finding me looking fixedly at the girl, she was observing me time & again. Then coming forward she straightway said, *"I presume you have come from Kolkata?"*

"Yes, I am from Kolkata."

"If I am not mistaken, you are the poet & litterateur uncle. Is it not?"

"Yes. But I can't recognize you."

"But I could recognize you at first sight uncle."

"Uncle! Do you know me?"

The girl said with a sweet smile, "I was sure you may not recognize me. Long days passed. OK, uncle, do you remember your yellow butterfly? I am that your yellow butterfly. Shabnam Mondal."

"Oh Gosh! I couldn't recognize you. You are Shabnam? My yellow Butterfly? Well, why did you come to Delhi? Is it for the World Book Fair?"

"Oh, that is a long story. I will tell you everything. Before that please tell me have you come to Delhi for a pleasant trip along with aunty?"

"Oh no. I have come to this World book fair, as invited my publisher. My latest novel **'Where the life dries out'** *published internationally and is being displayed here in the stall of my publisher. By the way, let me introduce you to my misses."*

As I introduced my misses with Shabnam, she promptly touched her feet in obeisance. As she tried to touch my feet, resisting her I asked, *"Leave it Shabnam. I can't listen to your story standing here. Better, let us go out of this hall to a restaurant. While drinking tea or coffee we will chit-chat."*

We came out of the hall. There were rows of restaurants. We enter a neat & clean restaurant ordered three cups of coffee & cakes.

While drinking coffee I asked Shabnam, *'Now you narrate your story Shabnam."*

"Certainly I will tell the episode. Before that please tell me, uncle, how did you enjoy the Delhi trip with aunty?"

"Oh no, I didn't come here for a trip. I came to Delhi in the World Bookfair at Pragati Maidan as invited by my publisher."

"Oh, what you say. Have that publisher published any of your books?"

"Yes. My latest novel 'Where the life dries out' published internationally by the publisher and is being displayed in the World Book Fair."

"So nice. I wish to read that novel."

"Now you narrate your anecdote."

"Uncle, you may remember I narrated my struggle of life to you while sitting in a tea stall at the Kolkata Book Fair.'

"Yes, I remember that. You were then a student at Kolkata University."

"Yes uncle, during that period I was residing in the house of Jakir Sahib at Park Circus. Highly educated & widower Jakir Sahib used to treat me & extend affection as his own daughter. In my life, Jakir Sahib appeared as the ambassador of Allah. He used to keep his affectionate attention to my comfortable board & lodging, study, etc. That's why he was open-handed for me in all respect. Initially, I was hesitant to accept financial assistance from him. But thinking that he might be pained by heart I accepted his financial assistance.

The final examination of the university was advancing. I concentrated solely on my studies. Observing me minutely, Jakir Sahib appointed a professor for tutoring me. That aged professor Pratul Bandopadhyay was a scholar & a good-hearted person. Because of his active association & proper guidance, I passed a master's degree in first class.

I intended to continue further studies but considering the financial constraint of my ammu & abbu I started applying for some job.

Jakir Sahib desired for my further studies to be continued. But perceiving the precarious financial condition of my ammu & abbu he advised me to assist them being their only child.

Due to my untiring effort as well as the active cooperation of Jakir Sahib I could get an appointment as a teacher in a private school in fat salary."

"Then what happened to your ammu & abbu? Did you bring them to you?"

"No uncle, that was not feasible at that period. I served as a teacher for about two years residing in the house of Jakir Sahib. After two years I purchased a small two BHK flat at Kalyani town & shifted my parents there. That time my abbu stopped driving the van. That was the first time my abbu was spending his leisure time in life. But my ammu didn't desire to quit the service in the nursery school. That's why I didn't compel them to come with me. They were spending their peaceful life as per the benediction of almighty Allah.

Besides teaching the students in the school, I used to tutor the students privately just to earn more money. My life was being spent following the beaten track.

Sitting in the school library I used to go through various journals, magazines & precious books. Thus once while going through a journal my eye was stuck at interesting news. It was a story of growing up struggling against the poverty of a daughter of a South Indian peasant. That girl being successful in IAS (Indian Administrative Service) posted as District Magistrate of Erode of Tamil Nadu. This story inspired me for the preparation of appearing in the IAS examination. I knew that the IAS examination is a hard nut to crack. But I succeeded in the examination at once chance.

My hard work has paid off and I am very happy. I credit my Allah above all, my parents, teachers, friends, and Jakir Sahib for success. I have come here to Delhi for two years of training. After completion of training, I will have to move to my own state where my posting as a District Magistrate will be decided by the state government."

My wife & I were listening dumb-folded to the anecdote of a girl struggling against all the antagonism, all the resistance of life.

Breaking our silence Shabnam said, *"Uncle now I will have to return to the campus. May I take leave of you?"*

"Ok, Shabnam. My good wishes & God's blessings will always be with you."

"Uncle & aunty when I will return to Kolkata, certainly your Yellow Butterfly will come to your residence to meet with you. Goodbye now."

We two came out of the restaurant. I was looking steadfastly at the outgoing Yellow Butterfly of mine. That Yellow Butterfly is now flying high in search of Paradise on earth.

I was spending days in a state of obsession. In an instant four days passed. Being fascinated by the hospitability of the hotel staff thanking them for hiring a taxi both of us arrived at New Delhi Station. Our birth was booked in the AC compartment. The Rajdhani Express set out in the afternoon. Gradually the Delhi station faded away. The darkness of evening was descending down. Taking aside the curtain from the window, I was enjoying the beauty of darkness the outside of the train. As soon as we consumed the tea/coffee with some snacks served by the waiters of Rajdhani express, the vegetarian meals for dinner were served. That was certainly vegetarian dishes for us.

At midnight putting off the lights, we started

welcoming the Goddess of slumber. The train was moving at her own speed.

"Iti Shri Sanjay Ubaacha"

(Here concludes the narration of Shri Sanjay)

Kanakanjali

Preface:

The human being may take birth in the indigent domestic life. But he or she may arise as a superhuman/woman with supernatural power due to dominance of will-force. The wave of His or her fragrance, her effulgence, her scintillation, her infallible humanity spreads all over the world. The gloomy lives of the countless patients were illuminated by the inundation of a beam of light.

Human life is mortal. But the mortality of human beings can be transformed into immortality through the performance of good & virtuous deeds. The credentials, the milestone of the glorious deeds of this celebrated person are being appeared in the world with the rising head.

Such as, the anecdote of virtuous deeds of a magnanimous lady was spread through the hearsay. I had a desire to catch a sight of the testimony of her various virtuous deeds but so far I couldn't find a convenient time. The opportunity came by the news of the ailment of one of my relations. I came to know he had been admitted to a hospital, which was my desired testimony of her good & virtuous deeds.

I didn't want to delay more. I rushed in the afternoon to have a look at that monument of good deeds.

<u>1st Chapter</u>

I was standing at a spot in front of which, resplendent with its head high a colossal hospital, known as *Kanakanjali Super-specialty Hospital*.

The name *Kanakanjali* is so much magnanimous that can be perceived from its intrinsic meaning. *Kanak* means Gold and *Anjali* means offering to the deity with folded palms.

Oh no! I am not a grammarian. I didn't sit here for explaining the grammar.

I had to come here to attend one of my distant relatives, who had been admitted to this super specialty hospital being attacked with cardiac arrest. *Oh! It's a glittering hospital!* It is not a governmental hospital but a private one. I entered the hospital. In front of me, there were two cubicles, one was of reception and the other was of the inquiry counter. Two pretty smart girls sitting at the counters were dealing with the patient party amiably. They were receiving & sending messages through computers. In front of counters, there were several cushioned chairs for the patient parties, waiting to visit their patients already admitted to the hospital. There were two lifts for going to the upper floors. One lift was reserved for the Doctors & ailing patients and the other for the patient parties. By the side of the lifts, there was a staircase. By the side of the staircase, there was one corridor. I walked through the corridor & peeped. There were several cubicles for Doctors' chambers on one side. There were a number of cushioned chairs/benches in the waiting hall. Several patients were waiting for their turn with their family members. On the opposite side, there was the number of cubicles with denotations e.g. Pathological Lab, ECG, ECHO cardiograph, X-ray unit, USG unit, etc. Scrutinizing minutely, I returned to the reception hall. The bell had rung time for visiting the patients. Enquiring the receptionists about the Cardiology Department, I came to know it is on the second floor. Patient parties were found entering the lift for going up. I had to wait until the lift coming down. Looking this & that way, my eyes stuck on a large photograph fixed on the wall. It was a portrait of an aged woman. She was the founder of this great multi-storeyed Super specialty hospital *Kanaknjali*. She was *Kanaklata*Das. I wonder about reading her short biography on the photograph. Being more inquisitive about learning more about her, I entered the lift.

Arriving on the 2nd floor I was not procrastinated to find out the ICU of the Cardiac Department. My relative already had bypass surgery & now he was shifted to ICU. But it was not easily accessible inside the ICU. The patient in ICU could be viewed from outside through the transparent glass fitted peephole. If somehow permission would have obtained, then keeping the shoe in the rack kept outside of the room, wearing the apron supplied by the ICU then was allowed to enter the ICU. Even then the patient party was not allowed to come in the vicinity of the patient in ICU. I did the same. Following all the procedure, entered in ICU. I observed that my relative after his bypass surgery was then in a deep slumberous state. Asking about the condition of my relative with the doctor & the nurse I came out of the unit.

I couldn't control my temptation to go around this beautiful, neat & clean, well-maintained gorgeous hospital.

I was achieving self-complacency in visual perception wandering around at various floors viewing the wards one after the other. I found that the surgical unit was present on most of the floors, which was known as Operation theatre.

I had seen the Emergency room, Obstetrics & Gynaecology Department for women patients, and Aesthetic & Reconstruction Surgery Department. Besides the Cardiac Department on the 2nd floor, I have seen one after the other the Oncology Department, (where there are Medical, Surgical & Radio Therapy wards present separately). On the upper floor there was Neuroscience Department, the Metabolic & Bariatric Surgery Department & on another floor there was the Bone Marrow Transplant Department, Urology Department, Nephrology Department & Kidney Transplant Department. Descending down on the ground floor I noticed other ancillary Services. Being struck dumb I became enchanted while observing those vast activities. I came to my senses in the words of a pretty young nurse. She said, *"Uncle, the time to visit the patient is over."* I came near the lift simpering. But unfortunately, the lift is closed. I had no other go but to come down through the staircase. Looking at the photograph of the lady on the wall, I was overwhelmed with ecstasy that who was that lady, who introduced this philanthropic institution so excellently.
Coming out of the reception hall I noticed some drug & medicine stores at some distance within the premises of the hospital.

Proceeding further towards the left side I noticed two underground garages. The smaller one was marked for Doctors, Nurses & hospital staff. The larger one was marked for the patients' parties. From the hospital entrance gate to everywhere the security staffs were very much alert. I found at all the floors, outer departments & outskirts of the hospital attached with CCTV cameras. It seemed that the hospital was well protected. All the floors & outer departments had fire extinguishers. Hospital had its own fire service department for fire fighting in case of emergency.

As I had been going around looking into the arrangements of the hospital, a security person suspecting my movement came & asked the reasons for my snooping. In reply, I clarified that I came to visit my relative. Now while going out I being fascinated was observing the hospital premises & didn't have any other intension. The security person smilingly told me that my movement was marked in the CCTV that's why he was questioning me. However, thanking him I came out of the hospital.

2nd Chapter

A somewhat big restaurant found on the opposite side footpath of the hospital. I read the name of the restaurant as *'Kanak smriti Mandir'* (which means Kanak memorial temple). *What a strange event! 'Kanakanjali' Hospital was in front of me & just opposite to it 'Kanak Smrity Mandir'! Then is there any connection between this restaurant with the hospital?* Slowly I went forward towards the restaurant. Once more I started reading the name of the restaurant. Yes, it is clearly written in large letters of alphabets *'Kanak Smrity Mandir'*. My inquisitiveness increased further. With a slow pace, I entered the restaurant. A neat & clean inner apartment was decorated with some interior decorating. There was a quadrangular table with four chairs on all sides. There were multitudes of similar tables. On one side there were small cabins separated by multi-colors curtains from the hall. Most probably these were preserved for some family members. Just by the side of the entrance, there was a wooden cabinet bedecked with beautiful artistry. That was the cash counter. A pretty young girl was sitting at the cash counter. A grey-haired old person was sitting by her side. It seemed the old person might be the owner of the restaurant. A gatekeeper in uniform with arms was standing at the entrance gate.

While observing the sceneries of the inner apartment a plate of canvass came to my notice behind the wall of the cash counter. It was a portrait of a woman. Being struck dumb I was going on looking at the portrait, which I noticed on the wall of the reception hall of the hospital. It was a similar portrait of majestic Kanaklata Das.

The dark black veil of the evening was gradually enveloping the area. Alike the illumination of the *'Dipavali'* festival, decorated with lightings was coruscating the visible *'Kanakanjali'* Super-specialty Hospital at the outside of the restaurant. The feeble greenish light created chiaroscuro in the inner apartment of the restaurant.

I kept gazing dumbfounded at the portrait of that magnanimous lady Kanaklata Das. All of a sudden I came to my senses with a suave touch of palm on my shoulder. Turning back I found that it was an affectionate touch of that grey-haired old person.

He asked me, *'Please take your seat. What do you like*

to have, tea or coffee, or any other eatables?"

I replied with a smile, *"For the time being please place an order for a cup of tea & one plate of cake."* As I sat occupying a chair, I noticed that the old person giving the order for a cup of tea & a plate of cake sat in a chair opposite to my chair.

While sipping my teacup, as I was looking at the portrait on the wall, the old person said, *"It seems that you are being astonished looking at that portrait here. Perhaps you are seized with suspicion about the similarity of the lady in this portrait with the photograph of a lady in the hospital."*

Nodding my head I said, *"You are correct. I am really surprised to observe the similarity of this portrait of a woman with the photograph of the majestic lady of the hospital. Is there any relation of this restaurant with that hospital?"*

The old person keeping silent for a while replied with a grave voice, *"No, you might have mistakenly understood. This restaurant doesn't belong to the progenitress of the hospital. Now a query may appear in your mind why then this similar portrait is kept here."*

"Of course. That thought is being circumambulated within my mind for so long. Then what is the reason to hang that portrait here? And why the name of this restaurant has denoted as 'Kanak Smriti Mandir'?"

The old person replied with pococurantism, *"The reason is all these are the relationship of self-esteem."*

"Self-esteem! How is it? Will you please tell me clearly?"

"Certainly I will tell. But if you have sufficient time then you will have to listen to the entire episode with patience."

"Of course I will listen to. I have enough time with me. I will set out after listening to the entire episode."

"In that case, it is better not to tell the anecdote in front of other customers. Please come with me to my annex. We will chit-chat

there."

Getting up from my seat as I went to the cash counter for paying the price of tea & cake, the old person refusing to accept the price, took me to the adjacent chamber. It won't be superfluous to say that this chamber was a small bedroom. Inside the room, there was a single bed cot, on which a white bed sheet. The pillow cover was also milk-white. A bedside table was kept by the side of the cot. A flower vase was placed over it. Some sticks of tuberose were kept in it. A Smartphone was also on the table. There were two cushioned rattan chairs. Costly white curtains were hanging from the windows & door. And what was most amazing that on the opposite wall of the pillow there was a well-framed photograph of Kanaklata Das. While sitting on the chair, staring at the photograph struck dumb, the old person said sitting on the cot, *"I have a self-esteem relationship with her. She is my inspiration for all activities."*

I said being flabbergasted, *"I couldn't get it, Sir."*

He replied with a smiling face, *"The memory which is concealed within the inner core of my heart can it be conceived so easily?"* Now after a while, he said in a normal voice, *"I Don't know your name so far. Let me introduce myself. My name is Mrityunjay Saha, a lifelong bachelor trader. And your name please."*

"I am Shri Sanjay, a writer."

"Writer! That's good. Certainly, my untold anecdote will be published as a novel."

"I will try that. Now let me listen to your untold anecdote."

"Yes. Indeed it is an untold anecdote. I never shared my story with anybody else. Observing you & your inquisitiveness, it came to my mind that revealing my stories to you let me be unburdened. But this story is not of mine. This is the story of Kanaklata Das. I also

became entangled with that anecdote.''

Now, the old Mritunjay babu looking for some time at the photograph of Kanaklata Das began his untold story with a choked voice heaving a deep sigh. I being an enchanted listener was listening to that intertwined memory of afflicted anecdote.

<u>3rd Chapter</u>

"The commencement of this doleful story is of long ago. That was 1947 AD. There was the partition of the country. The deluges of the displaced peoples from East Pakistan (Now Bangladesh) were going on thrashing on the West Bengal. Most of the refugees were compelled to take shelter in the reserved camps for refugees. And some of them took shelters in the residents of their relatives.

In such a way a dislodged from ancestral homestead, utterly ruined family losing once all in East Pakistan helplessly took shelter at the house of their distant relative. Sanjib Biswas was compelled to flee away to this country with his family members resorting to the accumulated amount obtained by selling the agricultural land property as far as possible. Being stable in the house of his distant relative, Sanjib babu set up a tea shop purchasing a piece of land spending some portion of his accumulated money. While selling in his teashop was flourishing, he constructed a hut to lay their heads in the adjacent land of the shop. Somehow his bare subsidence was being maintained along with his wife & only female child Kanaklata in their poverty-stricken domestic life.

Sanjib babu got his only daughter 12 years old Kanaklata in the fifth standard at the local primary school.

While studying in class nine at higher secondary school of the locality after completion of studies in the primary school, then Kanaklata was of sixteenth aged girl.

During that period Kanaklata became acquainted with one adolescent boy named Mrityunjay. Kanaklata was prompt & witty, soft-spoken, and benevolent of character. Bashful characteristic Mrityunjay became fascinated with these qualities of Kanaklata. The friendship grew between them. Kanaklata used to consider Mrityunjay as her own brother. Subsequently, Kanak taking away Mrityunjay to her hut thatched with tree leaves got him introduced to her parents.

Mrityunjay, destitute of parents was sheltered under a childless maternal uncle. Though he was an orphan yet he was an object of affection of his maternal uncle. As such uncle was attentive about the education & other matters of Mrityunjay.

Mrityunjay was enjoying the affectionate touch of his heavenly parent from the proximity of Kanaklata's parent. The parent of Kanaklata also used to treat Mrityunjay as their own son.

But unfortunately, the moderately wealthy maternal uncle & aunty couldn't approve of the intimacy of Mrityunjay with that ill-fated indigent family. Though Mrityunjay was prohibited by his maternal uncle to make intimacy with Kanak & family, yet Mrityunjay used to keep in contact surreptitiously with his country sister Kanaklata & her family members. But this news couldn't be suppressed further. The news reached in the ear of maternal uncle through the depraved hearsay of the neighbor. Even after several scolding, Mrityunjay couldn't be rectified then maternal uncle banished him from home. Being homeless destitute Mrityunjay leaving the home with some of his accumulated money & garments went to Kanak's parent explaining them about the situation. Kanak's father Sanjib babu & mother gave shelter to this filial son Mrityunjay.

The arrival of Mrityunjay became advantageous to Sanjib babu. The assistance of Mrityunjay in the tea shop reduced the working pressure on Sanjib babu. Mrityunjay applying tact & ingenuity made arrangements of selling omelets & toasts as well as hot fried chops & cutlets in addition to tea & cakes. Thus he attracted many people especially commuters. It became a profitable business.

The academic education of Mrityunjay became confined within the tenth standard of schooling because of his quitting the house of his maternal uncle. Since the thatched hut of Kanak & family was very small to accommodate Mrityunjay, hence he used to spend the night on the Railway platform.

Gradually this news of wretchedness of Mrityunjay reached in the ear of his maternal uncle through hearsay. Uncle considered himself as liable for such misery of his beloved nephew. Maternal aunty too became worried about the nephew. Both husband & wife arrived at the teashop. Both of them repeatedly tried to take him back home. Mrityunjay politely refusing them told that he wouldn't return home, since he got back the touch of affection of his deceased parent from Kanak's parent. Even after innumerable requests from maternal uncle & aunty observing his apathy to return to the domestic life of contentment, the couple secretly contacted Sanjib babu requested him to give monetary help for the construction of a brick-build house for them so that Mrityunjay need not spend the night in the platform.

Sanjib babu desired that Mrityunjay continue his studies. But considering the financial constraint of the family, Mrityunjay put an end to his studies.

Chintaharan babu the maternal uncle of Mrityunjay off & on used to arrive at the teashop just to take care of his own sister's son. He also desired that Mrityunjay begin his studies again. But Mrityunjay being employed himself intently in the business didn't incline him to begin studies.

In the meanwhile Chintaharan babu, the maternal uncle of Mrityunjay brought a matrimonial alliance to Sanjib babu for his daughter Kanaklata. Would be bridegroom was educated & well established in service. Sanjib babu accepted that alliance. After a long discourse with Chintaharan babu, it was decided that the father of the youth would come to the house of Sanjit babu to fix up the date of marriage.

Thus Kanaklata got married to Subrata Das before crossing the boundary line of the school. Sanjit babu bore the expanses of the wedding within the range of his financial capacity. Kanaklata entered in the domestic life of Subrata as a newly wedded wife. Subrata was in service in a jute mill as a supervisor. At home with his widow mother & bride Kanaklata he was spending days in delight.

But inevitable are the decrees of God. Just after two years or so, Subrata was affected by the severe ailment. Owing to his working environment in the jute mill, his lungs were affected by the floating dust of jute particles through inhalation. Along with respiratory trouble, he was gradually getting emaciated. The doctor of the jute mill after checking him thoroughly diagnosed that Subrata was affected with COPD. Subrata was referred to the Medical College Hospital, Kolkata. Thereafter various pathological tests & PFT, Doctor declared that Subrata was affected with lung cancer. While spending money on his treatment most of his accumulated money was exhausted. Then she had to live from hand to mouth.

There was heaping of sorrow upon sorrow. Kanaklata's parents expired within a short period. Kanaklata came to her parent's house for a funeral ceremony. Just then Mrityunjay came to know about the serious disease of Subrata. Considering the enormous expenditure in his treatment, Mrityunjay voluntarily assisted Kanaklata in giving some money. Though initially, Kanaklata didn't want to accept the money, yet due to compulsion, she had to accept the money. But she didn't want to embarrass Mrityunjay, a petty shopkeeper asking for money for her husband's treatment. Rather Kanaklata begged the doctors & nurses for free treatment of his husband folding her hands. But in vain. Unfortunately, no doctors or nurses extended their helping hands to the penniless Kanaklata.

*But the misfortune never comes alone.*In the meanwhile Kanaklata became pregnant. She delivered a male child at home with the active assistance of her neighbor. On one side was the expenditure for the treatment of her husband and on the other side spending money on the newborn baby. She was in great difficulties in managing the expenditures.

To bear the expenditures Kanaklata started tuition to the children. In this way, while pulling the domestic affairs with great difficulty, Subrata breathed his last without any treatment. Because of her son's premature death Subrata's mother being mentally broken down expired.

Kanaklata became unaccompanied on the earth. Her only viaticum was her newborn baby. Standing by the side of the flaming funeral fire she promised with tearful eyes that she won't allow any indigent persons to die without treatment alike her husband Subrata. Picking up a handful of ashes of the funeral pile, smearing on her forehead Kanaklata yelled, *"I will build up such a hospital, where all penniless peoples will get free medical treatment. I will have to somehow procure money for this mission of mine."*

That day onwards the foundation stone was laid within the sacred & secret abode of the heart of Kanaklata."

Saying up to this Mrityunjay babu getting up suddenly said, *"Please wait for a while. I shall come back just now."* Saying so, he left out of the room. Being spellbound, listening to the heartrending anecdote of Kanaklata Devi, with an afflicted mind I made obeisance to the photograph of Kanaklata Devi hanging on the wall.

In the meanwhile, Mrityunjay babu entering in the room with a tray containing two cups of tea & some pieces of cake, while sitting on the cot said, *"So far you were listening to the anecdotes with patience. That's why I brought this little tea & cake. While drinking the tea we will chitchat."*

"Oh no. Please don't worry about me. I am overwhelmed to listen to the anecdote of the struggle of life of this highly glorious lady. Please narrate, I will listen to".

"Yes. It was certainly a struggle for existence. Still, now you haven't listened to the entire episode. Once you listen to the entire story, then only you can perceive how a person can make the impossible one to possible one by perseverance."

While sipping the tea Mrityunjay babu began

narrating that anecdote of an unprecedented struggle of the existence of Kanaklata Devi.

<u>4th Chapter</u>

Kanak became sheer alone after the demise of her husband Subrata. Her only dependence was her year-aged male child. That solitariness remained as condensed black night within her heart. That solitariness was associated with extreme financial stringency.

Mrityunjay often used to come to her residence just to alleviate her solitariness. Mrityunjay desired that the sister Kanaklata would stay with him in his small house. But Kanaklata with implicit confidence replied, *"No brother no. I don't have any objection to stay with you. But relinquishing this shelter conferred by my husband my perception of penury will perish. The memory of my husband's death without proper treatment will be on the wane. Along with that the desire for the construction of a hospital meticulously nourished within my heart may become extinct. For that reason, I will have to stay permanently in this nook of the house."*

"But my sister, how will you bring up your child within this extreme penury? More so how will you construct your well-nourished hospital in mind?"

"Brother Mrityunjay, If there is a will, there is a way. I will try my level best to accumulate money for my mission. Somehow or rather, I will have to compile enormous money with the aim of construction of the hospital. I will devote myself in all respects for the construction of such a hospital, where the wretched penurious peoples will get benefited by cashless medical treatment."

"My dear sister, no doubt your mission is sublime. Please give me an

opportunity to participate in your great activities."

"Of course, without your active participation, my every stepping will become futile."

"It appears good to me. Now listen to me. You might have known that my maternal uncle Chintaharan babu & aunty expired a few years back. Before their demise, they bequeathed all of their movable & immovable property & bank balance in my name. But I remained in your parent's house & running my old tea shop by the side of the railway station. If you acquiesce then I can employ this wealth gifted by my maternal uncle in your highly glorious activities."

"No brother, please don't mind. I will construct that public hospital with my hard-earned money. But in the future, if it is required, I will inform you about that. Then you may invest your money in my hospital."

Mrityunjay could perceive that Kanaklata a woman with firm consciousness would never solicit money from anybody else in order to find out the achievement of her mission. But Mrityunjay inwardly determined to co-operate his sister Kanaklata in her every step to build up a hospital.

Mrityunjay returned to his home near the railway station with mental readiness to devote himself to the noble activities of sister Kanaklata. He engaged himself in the trading of a tea stall.

<u>5th Chapter</u>

Thereafter, a few months passed. He couldn't have information about Kanaklata. That's why once he arrived at the house of Kanaklata in the early morning. Entering the house he noticed that some male & female children sitting on the floor of the room were learning some lesions in some modulate voice. Obviously, they were the private students of Kanaklata. But Kanaklata was not at home. *"Where has she gone?"* Mentally anxious Mrityunjay asked the students engaged in reading, *"Do you know, where your teacher madam has gone?"*

A girl replied, "Yes, I just know. Our Kanak madam after tutoring us has gone to market."

"Market! In so early morning?"

"Yes. She goes there every day. Please go there you can meet her." The girl replied.

Without asking further Mrityunjay coming out of the room set out towards the local market.

Mrityunjay entering the market searched several points for Kanaklata. *"But where is Kanak?"* All of a sudden Mrityunjay noticed a large crowd engaged in purchasing the vegetables encircling a woman. Mrityunjay approached that place. Peeping through the crowd he became spell-bound. *"What's this?"* The vegetable seller was no other than Kanaklata. Pushing the crowd he came in front. Blooming youth Kanaklata was deeply engaged in selling the vegetable to the customers.

Mrityunjay noticed every one of the crowd was not the buyer. Some tender-aged youths were engrossed in achieving the closeness of the young woman Kanaklata. But the vegetable seller Kanaklata didn't have leisure time to give attention to those eve-teasers. She was going on selling the vegetables to the buyers. Mrityunjay observing everything asked her while kneeling down, *"Sister, what's the price of brinjal?"* Looking at the buyer Kanaklata startled, *"Brother Mrityunjay! When did you come?"*

"Just a few minutes back, I came here via your house. Will you come

now?"

"Oh yes. Today's job is over. Come on let's go."

While Kanaklata began winding up her articles for sale, the eve-teasers forthwith retreated from the place observing the presence of Mrityunjay.

While returning home Mrityunjay asked Kanak Lata, *"Sister Kanak, since when you started this selling of vegetables in the open market?"*

"It's just two months I just have taken part in this business. I find it is a profitable one."

"No doubt you're earning much from it, but have you noticed those flippant youths?"

"Yes, I keep my eyes on them. They are trying to become close to me."

"Don't you know they may harm you?"

"I just know. But you know, I need not give importance to them."

"OK, if you don't give importance to them. But if they besieging you try to harm you, what will you do?"

"Look, brother, these miscreants are mentally chicken-hearted. That's why they won't be able to outrage me. But even then if any one of them tries to outrage me unaccompanied. Then I keep a weapon always with me to impede them.' Saying so Kanaklata taking out a dagger from her bag said, *"So far I didn't have to use this weapon. For self-protection, I keep this always with me."*

"That, I can just see. But taking such a risk of life, why did you pick & choose such a below dignity profession?"

"Brother. I consider any manual labor as a dignified one. My principal object is to collect money for the construction of a hospital."

"But you could have earned more money tutoring more students in your house. Consequently, you wouldn't have to sell vegetables in the open market."

"Oh yes. That wouldn't be. But tutoring students at home whatever amount I can earn, that after spending on domestic affairs, a

negligible amount can be saved. That's why besides tutoring the students at home, I have chosen this profession for earning more amount. One more job I am going to start from the next month onwards. That is appointing me as a cook I am going to cook at various houses in the early morning. Thereafter going to market I will have to sell vegetables."

"Are you going to cook at different houses? Don't get utterly ruined Kanaklata. Moreover cooking in the houses, selling vegetables at the local market, when can you tutor your students then?"

"That I have already determined. Working from morning onwards naturally, I won't have time for tutoring. That's why I shifted my tutoring time in the evening."

"You will be engaged the whole day in your so many jobs. Then what will happen to your own baby? Where he will stay? What he will eat? Have you thought about these?"

"I have thought about all these aspects. You know a tender aged housewife stays in my neighboring house. Her name is Sakilabanu. She has a small baby. She only looks after my baby. She feeds him; she plays with him along with her own child. Again she lulls him to sleep. After returning home from my jobs, I pick my baby from her."

"Is it so? What's about Sakilabanu's husband? Is he in any job or business?"

"Who? Niyamat Bhai? He is working as a truck driver. He is a very pious, innocent & well-behaved person. In his house besides Shakila stays his old mother Nurunnesara begum. She is an aged woman of about seventy years. She fondles me as her own daughter and often comes forward to help me in any eventualities."

"Oh, then you say they are your strength & support. Is it not?"

"Yes. Besides that, I began selling vegetables in the open market in cooperation with Niyamat Bhai. Many persons in the market respect & are afraid of Niyamat Bhai. Those urchins of the market will

think twice before touching me. Niyamat Bhai already circulated in the market that I am his own sister. Hence everyone in the market keeps a respectful distance from me."

"That's good. It seems that Niyamat Bhai has much influence in this area. Is it not?"

"Yes, of course. It is not only for me, in case of danger & difficulties of others he extends his helping hand to them. He never acknowledges caste & creed. Just see about me. Niyamat Bhai only arranged those four houses, where I would have to cook. He already told those four houses not to disrespect me in any manner."

"Then when you are starting that cooking job?"

"That is from next month onwards."

"But when you will go for cooking, then who will cook in your house sister Kanak?"

"Why? I will cook. Getting up in early dawn, I will cook & keep it in the fridge. And the milk & baby food I hand over to Sakila regularly. She only looks after everything."

"I am overwhelmed by listening to this. It is fortunate to get such a good neighbor."

"You can say that. In this respect, I am really fortunate. That's why I have taken over so many jobs dependent on them."

"OK. But I must say something to you."

"What's that brother?"

"In this manner, you are working & the earning from that. For that, you will have to open a bank account to save all the earned money there."

"That is also arranged, brother. Niyamat Bhai opened a new bank account in my name taking me to a local bank."

"Bravo! Too good. Well, one more thing. Your husband Subrata before his demise where he was working, did that Jute authority paid his provident fund & Gratuity amount to you?"

"Yes, they delivered the amount to me Niyamat Bhai with a

persistent request to the leaders of union pressurizing the authority realized some amount. That amount was deposited in the local post office. Whatever amount I am getting from that as an interest, that is sufficient for my subsistence."

"In that case, do you deposit the amount in the bank, whatever you earn from tutoring the students as well as from the profit after selling the vegetables?"

"Yes. In the first week of every month, I go to the bank to deposit the earned money. This deposited money is the viaticum of the foundation of the hospital of my dream."

"As much as I am listening to you that much I am becoming overwhelmed. But I want a word from you. I know that initially, I won't get the opportunity to spend money on this commendable work. But I will take the responsibility of selecting the proper land for the erection of the hospital."

"Oh! Of course; Of course. But now it is like 'To count chickens before they are hatched.' We will have to wait for unlimited days for that. As & when some lump sum amount found to be in the bank, we will start the work."

"That of course right. By all means, I will start making inquiries about suitable land. Have you got any objections about that?"

"Not at all. Why should I have an objection in this respect? Well brother you go on searching for the land now itself."

After concluding their conversation for the day, Mrityunjay handing over the toys, baby suits & baby foods to Kanaklata brought for her baby took leave of her.

<u>6th Chapter</u>

In an instant five years passed. Just to get the whereabouts of his sister Kanaklata, Mrityunjay off & on pays a visit in the house of Kanaklata. In meanwhile a lot of changes occurred in the lifestyle of Kanaklata. Mrityunjay finds that Kanaklata still sells vegetables in the local market but not sitting by the side of the passage in the market. She sells vegetables sitting in a vegetable shop. That shop has been purchased by Kanaklata in the benevolence of Niyamat Bhai for one year. Mrityunjay observes more that Kanaklata has not to go for cooking from door to door. Instead, she has begun a home service. Cooking at home she supplies to the door to door as per customer's choice. One local boy has been appointed by Niyamat Bhai as a carrier of food materials.

Initially, Kanaklata had to cook herself alone. But of late a separate cook has to be appointed since the numbers of customers has been increased. After finishing the preliminary cooking, handing over the final cooking to the cook, Kanaklata sets out towards the marketplace after sending her son to school dressing up for school. Yes, Rajat Shubhra the son of Kanaklata is a student of the 2nd standard in the local school.

After the departure of Kanaklata to the market, her neighbor Sakilabanu takes care of the cooking. Sakila's son Rahaman too goes to school along with Rajat Shubra. Both of them are a student in the same class. Niyamat Bhai accompanies them to & fro to school.

When the sun rises in the mid sky, Kanaklata returns from the market to home. Rajat Shubhra also returns from school. After lunch taking momentary rest, Kanaklata becomes busy in the afternoon sitting. Sitting means tutoring the students. Rajat Shubhra and Sakila's son Rahaman too sit to study along with other students. That is not only the dry curriculum, besides that various types of children games are conducted, followed by the brightening of the party with songs & dances. Sakilabanu being a good singer & a mature dancer assists Kanaklata in this regard.

Mrityunjay on certain days spending the whole day in the house of Kanaklata becomes overwhelmed by observing the industriousness of Kanaklata.

Mrityunjay considers himself a favorite of fortune getting a diligent sister like Kanaklata. He returns to his home with a happy memory.

7th Chapter

The days are drifting away in the efflux of time. Months after months, years after years are get through accompanying the compound of weal & woe. So many memories are lost; countless memoirs are implicated in the way of livelihood.

Waking up in the crimson glow of the rising sun at dawn Kanaklata perceives that she has left behind a further decade of her life.

Her life as a vegetable seller has not begun to ebb. Still, now her cooking service center at home exists as well as the assembly of tutoring of the students as usual.

In an instant Rajat Shubhra, Kanaklata's son grows up. Sixteen-year-old Rajat Subhra & Rahaman are now the students of the twelfth class. Rajat Shubhra is regarded as a talented student at the school. The school authorities as well as Kanaklata have immense faith & expectation on the possessor of the first position in all the examinations Rajat Shubhra that this boy will once glorify their face.

Mrityunjay visits regularly to inquire about his sister

Kanaklata. He asks Kanaklata, *"Sister Kanak, what is your desire to put Rajat in which academic education after his schooling?"* *Kanak smilingly replied, "I have several high thoughts about him as a mother. But it's wise to ask him what my son desires to study, what he intends to be in life."*

As Rajat comes forward, Mrityunjay affectionately caressing him on his head asks, *"What's your desire to take which academic career after schooling? What you intend to be in your life?"*

Rajat without any hesitation replied sharply, *"I desire to be a doctor with a mission to serve the ailing patients."*

"Bravo! That's good. I desired the same reply from you internally."

That day Mrityunjay returned home with a happy memory.

<u>8th Chapter</u>

Sheer alone Mrityunjay has no knowledge of when he slept away while lying down on the bed building the castle in the air in the darkness of night. Being in a deep slumberous state Mrityunjay awakes by the sounds of hue & cry outside of his house. He kicks & caper to get up on the bed. *"What's the matter? What happened in so early morning?"* He comes out of the house putting on the room sandal. He notices some crowd gathered near the railway track. Proceeding further before asking the viewers he notices a blood-stained body of a young woman lying on the railway track.

He could perceive that the girl committed suicide jumping below the up train in the early morning. *"But why? Why this pretty life has chosen this sequel?"* Mrityunjay comes to know from the hearsay that the youth has cohabited with this girl from an indigent family promising to get her married. The girl became pregnant, the youth refused to marry her. That's why this sequel.

The entire crowd burst into a rage on the culprit youth. Police arrive. A suicide note is obtained by the side of the dead body. Police send the mortal body for post mortem.

Such an accident in the early morning saddened the heart of Mrityunjay. This fine morning becomes gloomy. He enters the room. He is not having the intention to open his tea shop because of that sad affair. He feels that this fatal incident in the morning is bringing some inauspicious hint.

That sorrowful incident of the morning weighed down the heart of Mrityunjay. He opens his tea shop reluctantly. The crowd of regular customers started gathering in the morning. Sitting on the benches kept in front of the tea shop the veterans giving the order for tea are discussing the present political situation as well as about the present cricket match while sipping the tea. Some of them are using the scurrilous comments on the morning painful incident. All the discussions are entering the auditory passage of Mrityunjay without being taking part in the discussion.

At about twelve-thirty noon shutting the tea shop, while taking lunch after taking bath, Mrityunjay listens to a sound of a knock on the door. *Who has come during this odd hour?'* saying so opening the door he finds that Rajat Shubhra standing at the door.

"What's the matter? Why you are here at this time? Any problem with Kanaklata?"

Some inauspicious apprehension makes him anxious.

"No uncle no problem with mummy. My mummy sent me to inform

you about the evil news."

"Evil News! What happened?"

"Uncle, our Niyamat uncle is hospitalized being injured in a road accident. Mummy asked you to come there."

"Oh, God! As if the inauspicious incidents are going on happening from morning onwards. Come on let us move now."

Mrityunjay along with Rajat Shubhra boarding in a taxi when arrived at the residence of Kanak, a plaintive cry was emanating from a house at the vicinity of Kanak's residence. After getting down from the taxi, Rajat Shubhra says, *"Uncle most probably my mummy has gone to the house of Niyamat uncle. Let us go there."*

As soon as they entered the premises of Niyamat's residence opening the entrance gate, Mrityunjay noticed many afflicted peoples are standing in the courtyard. The dead body of Niyamat Bhai is lying on the veranda. A police officer & two police constables are investigating the situation. Mrityunjay approaches the police officer along with Rajat Shubhra. On asking the police officer replies that while saving a private car from the opposite side, Niyamat's truck collided against a roadside tree. Consequently, Niyamat & his assistant got hurt. Niyamat's injury was grave. That's why on the way to the hospital he expired. After the post-mortem, his body has brought to his residence. The deposition eyewitnesses were taken by the police. There no fault of both parties. This is a mere accident only. The damaged truck of Niyamat has brought here.

Noticing the presence of Mrityunjay, Kanaklata coming out of the room breaks into wailing. A custodian on her head has expired. Mrityunjay starts consoling

Kanaklata.

<u>9th Chapter</u>

Several years passed after the demise of Niyamat Bhai. There is no change in the hackneyed life of Kanaklata. Her engagement in works begins at dawn after getting up from bed. Arranging the cookery of different items as per the choice of the customers at home service she sets out towards the vegetable market. While sitting in the vegetable shop selling the vegetable time passes past. During leisure time in between the selling, she breaks fast with snacks brought from home. As soon as the wall clock of the market sounds a gong of twelve-thirty noon, she shuts up the mat door & sets out towards her home. Sakilabanu the bibi of deceased Niyamat fully devoted herself to the cookery in the home service at the residence of Kanaklata. Besides that Sakilabanu has a particular work to prepare Rajat Shubhra & Rahamat for going to Medical College for studies after feeding them the heavy breakfast.

Yes, Rajat Shubhra & Rahamat are regular students of Medical College. Kanaklata had a deep-rooted desire to make her son a successful physician. Her concealed desire is going to be fulfilled soon. Along with him, she desired to make Rahaman, the only son of deceased Niyamat Bhai also a successful physician. Mrityunjay was very much endeavoring to metamorphose that dream of Kanaklata. By the untiring effort & secretly financial assistance Rajat Shubhra & Rahaman got the opportunity in studying medicine getting through the entrance examination.

Rajat Shubhra desires to become a successful Cardiologist in the future. That's why he is proceeding with mental preparation. On the other hand, Rahaman has a desire to become an Orthopaedic surgeon in the future. In order to encourage their mental desire, there were no faults & failings of Mrityunjay.

That's why at one day the hidden desires of two friends became embodied successfully. Rajat Shubhra joined Medical College as a Cardiologist. And Rahaman opened a private chamber in the town as an Orthopaedic Surgeon.

The motherly hearts of Kanaklata & Sakilabanu became overwhelmed with joy observing the establishment of their offspring as successful physicians.

But the journey of Kanaklata didn't stop here. In order to make successful of her long daydream to establish a new hospital, Kanaklata plunged herself with fresh enthusiasm. And in this noble act of Kanaklata, Mrityunjay devotes himself with heart & soul.

10th Chapter

And at last that opportune moment arrived. The auspicious moment to materialize the long waited dream is being manifested. Hunting for suitable land to establish the hospital was going on for a long. But unfortunately, no such land of choice was found. But Mrityunjay didn't lose his heart. He didn't become disheartened. He was going on trying.

Meanwhile, once Mrityunjay had been to a remote place of the Sundarbon area on a pleasure trip along with his friend circle under the custodian of a travel agency. Keeping the greenwood forest at both sides of the river Matla, the promenade boat was progressing further ahead. The travelers of the boat became extremely jubilant catching sight of a Royal Bengal Tiger busy in drinking water by the side of the river within the deep extending forest. But the travelers were desisted from making hue & cry in order to attract a glance of the royal tiger as directed by the travel agency. Only cameras of some of the travelers were making soft clicking noise to capture the picture of the bodily grace of the emperor of the greenwood forest.

The precarious condition of the residents of that place appeared in the mind of Mrityunjay during that pleasure trip.

At the termination of their pleasant trip, Mrityunjay decided to stay for a few days in the remote village. He expressed his desire to his friend circle & the travel agency. Accordingly, he intended to stay in a hotel in a small suburb neighboring the village.

He used to set out on a journey to the distant villages of the area. He used to make inquiries about the residents of the villages. He noticed most of the inhabitants were stricken with poverty. To earn their livelihood they used to catch fishes & crabs in the river within the woods, irrespective of males & females. Getting whatever little amount after selling those commodities to the middlemen in suburbs, they used to purchase commodities like rice, pigeon-pea, oil, etc for their bare subsistence.

While catching the fishes in the river within the deep forest or loping the branches of the tree in the forest they are involved in innumerable numbers of dangers. Some of them die by snakebite, some become prey of the tiger.

They neither have a very firm roof over their head nor any minimum facility of medical treatment. There is no accounting for how many villagers die out of malnutrition or without any treatment. If any pregnant woman is in travail, she has to be carried to a hospital 20/25 miles away lying on a rural cot. Else some midwife delivers the woman in her home only by the crude method.

While observing & listening to these episodes Mrityunjay felt affliction for these villagers. A thought started floating in his mind that if a hospital can be erected near these villages they will be benefitted getting proper treatment. Realizing the episodes of the pathetic tale of the villagers Mrityunjay returned to his house at Sodpur. Though he used to open the tea shop but unable to concentrate on work. The portrait of the faces of the poverty-stricken villagers floats in the mind of Mrityunjay every now & then. He conceives that some arrangements must be made for these villagers. Instantly he recalls the dream of Kanaklata for establishing a hospital.

Mrityunjay was spending days with an unstable mind. That's why he set out on a Sunday in respect of the residence of Kanaklata.

Kanaklata is quietly listening to the episode of the affliction of the villagers of the remote villages. Drops of tears roll down from her eyes through the cheeks. After narrating the entire episode Mrityunjay sits with a distressed heart looking at the face of Kanaklata. Overcoming her emotional state Kanaklata says to Mrityunjay, *"Brother, take me to those remote villages in the next Thursday. I want to percept visually all those afflicted rural peoples. I want o listen to their state of affliction with my own ears."*

"But sister Kanak, why Thursday? We can start tomorrow."

"Yes, that we can. But there is an auspicious moment on Thursday. That's why we should proceed for any auspicious work in some auspicious moment."

"OK, That's all right. But whether your son Rajat Shubhra will also accompany us ?"

"No. He has a special class at Medical College. He & Rahaman will go to college together. Sakilabanu will take care of them."

<u>11th Chapter</u>

Mrityunjay babu narrating the anecdote of an unprecedented struggle of the existence of Kanaklata Devi continuously pauses for a while. He says to me, " *Sanjaybabu, excuse me. Please wait for a while. I will come back shortly. I will have to look after my restaurant too."* Saying so Mrityunjay babu leaves the room.

Sitting alone in the room I was going on looking at the portrait on the wall. It was the portrait of that magnanimous lady Kanaklata Das. That portrait of the lady seems to be a live fairy looking at me with a sweet smile. I began recapitulating the anecdote so far I listened to from Mrityunjay babu. What a struggling life of that godly woman! She began her life from a big zero, without any helping hand, scarcity of money to maintain her day-to-day livelihood. Yet she never lost her courage. She never begged for any money from anybody else. She began earning money from selling vegetables in the open market. She started accumulating money in her bank account for her dream to establish one hospital, treating mostly indigent peoples free of cost. For earning more money for that auspicious mission as well as for the education of her only child, she started a home service delivering the food material to the people of the locality. By God's grace a good-hearted neighbor Niyamat, a truck driver, extended his helping hand to her in every aspect. He became her Godbrother.

Her high & only mission was to restore the poor sick peoples to health without charging a single penny from them. With my folded palm I bowed to that great lady.

Instantly Mrityunjay babu enters the room with two cups of coffee & some snacks.

Offering the cups & snacks to me he says, *"Sanjay babu, in my absence you might be feeling bored. Please excuse me for that. Since I will have to look after my business too, I have to go out often from you."*

"Oh no. I didn't feel any boredom here. I was recapitulating the anecdote so far I heard from you. Now please continue the rest of the story."

"Yes, I will begin the story. Before that, let us consume coffee & snacks first."

Both of us started seeping the coffee.

Once more looking at the portrait of that great lady, Mrityunjay babu starts narrating the interesting anecdote.

12th Chapter

Mrityunjay babu took Kanaklata to the remote villages just to get the practical situation of the rural area. Kanak moving around the villages, talking with the rural women & male could perceive their distressed condition. While talking with them since it became evening Kanaklata decided to spend the night in the hut of a fisherman. The wife of the fisherman served the best possible food to them cooked by her in her rural way.

Spending night with this indigent fisherman's cottage she could feel deeply about their way of life, their food materials, insufficiency of nutritious foods for the rural children & dearth of education, hygienic way of living, and especially the rural way of treatment. Perceiving the rural lifestyle of those remote villages, Kanaklata said with an afflicted heart, *"Dada (Elder brother) spending one night with these indigent people, what experience I have that is really painful. Probably we may not be able to reduce their entire distress & poverty. But I won't allow them to die without proper treatment. I will establish such a hospital on the outskirts of the township, where I will be able to serve these feminizing indigent rural peoples with proper medical assistance without charging a single penny. Dada, you search for a befitting land for establishing the hospital."*

"That's it. I will remain in close touch with the availability of proper land. Now for the time being let us go back home."

Kanaklata & Mrityunjay returned home. Kanaklata returned with a heavy heart. Mrityunjay returned with a promise to find out a suitable land for the establishment of the desired hospital.

On her arrival at home, Rajat Shubhra & Rahaman came running with Sakilabanu to Kanaklata just to know the outcome of her journey to the remote villages. As asked for Kanaklata narrated her sad experience about the indigent villagers of remote villages. Listening to this episode, Rajat Shubhra & Rahaman promised that they would serve those poor rural people in all respects of medicinal treatment. Sakilabanu enquired about the availability of suitable land for establishing the hospital. Kanaklata replied that Mrityunjay would search about that.

13th Chapter

After the innumerable efforts, inexhaustible inquiry & search by Mrityunjay, acres of barren lands were found available adjacent to the suburb. Mrityunjay in company with Kanaklata arrived at the spot & showed her the barren land. Kanaklata liked & approved that land. After negotiation with the state authorities & completion of all the formalities, Kanaklata signed the deeds & documents to acquire the land.

Becoming a widow at the age of 18 years, which latent dream Kanaklata preserved for 30 years to establish a hospital promoting public welfare, now advanced one step forward on the way to reality.

In an auspicious day, Kanaklata, Mrityunjay, Sakilabanu, Rajat Shubhra & Rahaman arrived at the land along with the priest. The rural people were also invited to be present on the occasion of *"Bhumi Pujan"*(Veneration of Land). Kanaklata with the assistance of some villagers laid the foundation stone.

After the ceremony Kanaklata along with Mrityunjay, Rajat Shubhra, Rahaman & Sakilabanu distributed the 'Prasad', a small amount of money & clothes to the villagers present on the occasion. Villagers were so much happy that they chanted *"Kanak Mata ki Jai"*. But Kanaklata didn't like this chanting in her name. She prevented and said, *'Brothers & sisters, this land is for the establishment of a hospital, which will help you people for treatment free of cost. I am a representative of you all.*

Hence chanting in my name is not correct. If you at all want to chant, chant in the name of almighty God, who will give you strength & endeavor to establish this hospital within the shortest possible time."

Responding to the lengthy solicitation of Kanaklata, the villagers nodded their heads and began praying to their own adorable Gods of religious faith. Mrityunjay said, *"That's it. I pray to Mother Durga, the Goddess of strength, power & peace, to take care of you all & us. She will give mental strength to us to complete this hospital in the shortest possible time."*

14th Chapter

Narrating up to this Mrityunjay babu getting up from the cot, pours drinking water in the tumbler from a jug kept on the table. Gulping the water repeatedly asks me *"Sanjay babu like to drink water?"*

"Oh no. Just now I drank coffee. Thank you. You drink please."

"Oh yes. Let me drink some more water. This is my bad practice. I have become aged you know. Frequently my throat gets dried."

"It's natural, especially for aged persons. But one reason for frequent drying of the throat is rise of blood sugar. Did you ever got tested your blood?"

"No. Since long I couldn't get tested my blood sugar. Good, you have reminded me. Now I will get my blood tested."

"Not only blood sugar, but you will also have to give a blood sample for pathological examination like lipid profile, TC, DC, ESR, etc., as many as possible. Besides that you get your blood pressure checked as also ECG too."

"Ah! Sanjay babu! You are not only a writer. You have knowledge of pathological terms too!"

"No no. It's not like that. This is a common matter. Many persons

have knowledge about this."

" That may be. But you know? I have been engaged in this restaurant throughout the day, I don't get time to think about my health."

" You have become aged. Now you will have to take care of your health. You need not go out of the restaurant for your pathological examinations of your blood. You said that the only son of Kanaklata Devi is a cardiologist of this hospital. Is it not?"

"Yes, yes. Rajat Subhra and Salika's son Rahaman are doctors of this hospital. They often make a visit to this restaurant to have a cup of tea & inquire about me."

"That's good. Next time when they will come, please tell them about your blood examination. They will send somebody from the hospital to draw a sample of blood from you for testing in their pathological laboratory. Even they will measure your blood pressure as well as take your ECG here itself."

"Many many thanks. I never thought about this facility. This time I will get my blood tested. Whatever it may be. While talking about my physical problems, we have been diverted from the original topics. Well, what was I talking about?"

"You were narrating about the "Bhumi Pujan" (Veneration of Land) after purchasing the land for establishing the hospital. Thereafter what happened? You began the construction work of the hospital?"

As I ask him about that, Marityunjay babu smiling in gloomy face heave a deep sign looking at the photograph of Kanaklata Devi hanging on the wall, says, *'Noh! It was not so easy to lay bricks for construction."*

'Why? Was there any administrative problem?"

'Oh no. There were no administrative riddles. Rather, we got all assistances & supports from the administration."

'Then, what's the trouble?

"Sanjay babu there is is a saying, 'Man proposes God disposes'."

Thereafter, Mrityunjay babu introduces what anecdote, that is really extremely distressing, most pathetic heart-rending one.

<u>15th Chapter</u>

Yes, there is a saying, **"Man proposes God disposes of."** But why God will dispose of human desire, especially virtuous design? God, may not like or may not approve any desire of self-conceitedness or any wicked desire. But God won't dispose of the goodwill & beneficence of others, heartfelt emotion towards distress & poverty of wretched peoples to drive away their distress. Rather, He will bless to execute the will well. That's why He will whole heatedly desire for the good execution of any endeavour of any charitable work. Then why the endeavour of Kanaklata Devi to establish a charitable hospital for the indigent villagers was impeded? Why then strong gale came down on earth with a loud roar of nature?

Behind the fury of nature certainly, there was some abstruse mystery in the mind of God. That's why the construction work of the hospital was momentarily obstructed!

Strokes after strokes of immeasurably hurricanes, 'Bulbul', 'Hudhud', 'Aila' by name had to be endured by the inhabitants of 54 islands. Wind speed is about 175 -180 Kmph damaged several houses partially, mud-walled huts were totally smashed. Since the advance arrangement was made by the State Government to shift the most of the habitants to safer places in some schools converted to rehabilitation centres. Several naval relief teams were deployed in the Sundarbons region where many villagers were marooned by flooding by seawater & rivers. National Disaster Response Force was deployed for relief operations. The extent of damage would be beyond repair. Some relief camps were established by the Government. During this disaster, there was political parties' turmoil began while distributing relief to these distressed people. Some NGOs like *'Bharat Sevashram Sangha'*, Ramkrishna Mission' came forward to help these villagers on spot.

Such is the life of inhabitants of the Sundarbon area. Besides the above strokes of tempests, they are to encounter against Royal Bengal tigers, fight against the sudden snap of the poisonous snakes, struggle against the crocodile in the river, endure the poverty, struggle against the deluge. While fighting against all these natural courses of events either they submit to death or battle of their life along with unbearable pain.

Such a mighty dreadful tempest thrashed against the ground of the state. The lives of inhabitants disrupted turning topsy-turvy. Large trees were uprooted tearing asunder electric cables falling on the electric lines. Uprooted several light poles. Roads of the township were obstructed. Township & suburbs were in deep darkness at night. State Government & Army personals rushed to bring the normalcy of township & suburbs.

This is about the chronicle of the township lifestyle of the metropolis.

But which strong wind, which whirlwind blew over the rural lives of villages or islands adjacent to Sundarbon, who are keeping the account of that? Well-arranged hard-earned domestic lives were shattered to pieces by the strokes of the hurricane, which person of the township will sympathetically feel for that?

Yes, there are some people who are compassionate to the peoples stricken with adversity, who are afflicted with the misery of others. Those peoples perceive with their indwelling spirit about the poverty-stricken peoples. These types of people with felling pain at another's affliction are a handful in society.

And Kanaklata Devi was among these peoples beneficial to the public. That's why she spent a night in the thatched hut of an indigent fisherman just to perceive by senses about the struggle for existence of the poverty-stricken rural peoples.

That tender-hearted Kanaklata Devi after visualizing the frantic affair of cyclone in her township could perceive the extreme miseries of the villagers or dwellers of the islands adjoining the Sundarbon.

She was collecting news of the dilapidated villagers of the villages & islands engulfed by the severe whirlpool or deluge sometimes through Mrityunjay or sometimes through her son Rajat Shubhra.

The paddy fields were inundated with salty seawater due to the crumbling down of earthen dykes. Corps was decomposed coming in contact with salty seawater. Innumerable huts made of mud were razed to the ground. The fishermen were sustained to lose due to the utterly spoiling of their fishing accessories. Some of the fishermen were missing due to the drowning of fishing boats in the deep sea.

You know East wildlife sanctuary of Sundarbon extends over an area of 31,227 hectares where Sundari trees dominate the flora, interspersed with Gewa, Passur trees, etc. It is important to mention about Goran trees grew in the most saline areas, which protects Sundarbon from Natural calamities. But unfortunately, some miscreants illegally cut the trees. Due to the severe whirlwind, these protectors of Sundarbon were thrashed on the ground affecting the lives of the villagers.

Homeless, resource less & utterly helpless rural peoples got a temporary place in the tents donated by the state govt. Many villagers didn't acquire that much fortune. Most of them had only a piece of tarpaulin over their head. What a precarious condition! Besides that, there was feud between political parties in connection to the distribution of relief. In between this mutual competition of political parties, came forward the NGOs like "Bharat Seva Shram Sangha" carrying milk, Biscuits, for the children, flattened rice, bottles of drinking water, clothes, etc for the unfed, fasting villagers.

Motherly Kanaklata Devi's heart was overwhelmed with anxiety for the provision of foods for the fasting homeless villagers. She desired to go in person to the villagers stricken with adversity. Since that was not possible due to various reasons, she was prevented. That's why she handed over many garments, dry food materials, bottles of drinking water in the hand of 'Bharat Seva Shram Sangha' to distribute among the villagers.

16th Chapter

In an instant a year passed. The wound of unendurable stormy weather left behind in the livelihood of the villagers stricken by tempest was not so easily round. Gradually the fresh lease of lives was being established, small cottages in rows were being developed, due to the cooperation of the state or central Government, as well as by the generosity of some NGOs. Again the cultivation began after baling out the saltwater from the land. The fishermen in zeal afresh sailed their boats in the deep sea in order to catch fishes.

Vivification of life in the dying dwellers of Sundarbon was started.

During this period the long nourished dream of Kanaklata Devi began embodiment. Besides the establishment of the hospital, afresh endeavor appeared within the inner core of her heart. Kanaklata Devi perceived that these indigent villagers spend their day-to-day life in hardship in the small tent or a piece of a tarpaulin after being homeless during each & every natural calamity. During that period if they get some shelters within the brick-built houses they may get some relief.

That's why along with the erection of the hospital a rehabilitate center was also being erected.

A multi-storied hospital was constructed by the untiring efforts, active assistance of some of the villagers as well as the active participation of Mrityunjay babu. And a rehabilitation Centre came up not far away from the hospital.

Presumably, in order to establish one shelter for the homeless villagers during natural calamities, God delayed the construction of the hospital creating stormy weather.

17th Chapter

Mrityunjay babu keeps quiet for a few moments looking at the photograph of Kanaklata Devi, hanging on the wall. I could perceive looking at his dreadfully gloomy & dark face that there is a sign of appearance of the gale in his depth of heart. I could perceive that this gale is not any destructive gale but a gale of heartbreaking affliction. This gale is a gale of losing own kith & kin. That's why; I too without asking anything looked at the photograph of Kanaklata Devi steadfastly.

I don't know how long we were looking at the photograph. Both of them returned to senses by the call of the waiter of the restaurant.

Mrityunjay babu asking the waiter to go, says to me, *"Sanjay babu, please wait a bit. I am to look after the restaurant side too. I will come back soon."*

After a while, Mrityunjay returns with two cups of tea in hand.

"Please drink tea."

"Oh! You have brought tea again?"

"You know, there is no count of how many teas I drink throughout the day. That's why. How can I drink tea alone? I brought a cup for you too. Please drink it with me."

After completion of the chapter on drinking tea, I say to him *"So, finally the hospital was built?"*

"Yes, built. But what structure you are observing now, that mush was not constructed then. Then the hospital didn't come to the stage of Super Specialty hospital. But what's in that? With this magnanimous creation of Kanaklata, the welfare of the poor people spread at various points of compass orally by the people. Getting the information various News Channels thronged into the spot. Social media spoke at length about these activities of a hospital promoting

public welfare. The personal interview of Kanaklata was telecasted live.

Governor was invited to inaugurate the hospital. Governor humbly informed that he would positively be present at the inauguration ceremony. But the magnanimous inauguration would be done by Kanaklata Devi.

I got one marble tablet made. The name of Kanaklata Devi, the inaugurator was engraved in golden letters. The tablet was fixed on the outer wall of the hospital. A day for the inauguration was scheduled on an auspicious day. A colored canopy was pitched. The invitation was sent to the villagers."

"Did you not invite the Chief Minister of the state?" I interrupted Mrityunjay babu in between his talk.

"Is it ever possible that? Chief Minister & some of the ministers were also invited.

Thereafter on that auspicious day, the hospital was inaugurated. Chief Minister couldn't attend the inauguration since he had to attend some important meetings in Delhi. But before leaving the state he sent a benedictory letter & flower bouquet to Kanaklata through the Minister of the health of the state.

Kanaklata never liked to display herself ostentatiously. That's why she didn't accept the invitation from some TV Channels for a live show. But the splendor of the gleam of the bright sun couldn't be concealed.

Hence, the fame of this philanthropic Hospital while spreading arrived at the levee of Delhi. Kanaklata was honored by the President of India. Listening to this story of the great creation of Kanaklata many generous persons, many NGOs began sending voluntary donations to the hospital of Kanaklata. Initially, she was disinterested to accept these donations, but after convincement by Rajat Shubhra & me, she didn't object.

Those donation amounts were utilized to the uplifting of the hospital. Some portions of the donation amount were spent to construct the rest house for the night stay of the patient parties. A portion of the donation amount was utilized for the development of the rehabilitation center.

I too I utilized all the money donated to me by my maternal uncle in the construction of this restaurant."

"Did you give this name of this hospital as 'Kanakanjali'?"

"No, that naming of the hospital was after long days. Kanaklata never liked to display her name ostentatiously. But she named many wards e.g. Subrata Ward in her late husband's name, Niyamat Ward, in the name of Sakila's late husband, female ward as Sakila Ward, obviously in the name of her friend Sakilabanu. Kanaklata desired to name some ward against my name, but I objected to that.

But immutable is the degree of fate. She couldn't endure so much stress on her health. Kanaklata She became sick. She was admitted to the female ward of this hospital. But her cardiac problem was going on increasing. Renowned Cardiac surgeons attended took care of her. Bypass surgery was done.

Everything was precisely alright. Kanaklata was shifted to ICU. Kanaklata was under the special care of a Cardiac Surgeon. Several letters praying for the quick recovery of Kanaklata Devi reached. The Chief Minister of the state visited Kanaklata from outside of the ICU and left wishing her recovery.

Kanaklata was gradually recovering from the ailment. But what has happened! Once at night violent rainstorms started. There was a severe thunderbolt. In the morning when the rainstorm stopped, I had been to Hospital. I noticed that the Cardiac Surgeon was standing with some Cardiologists inside the ICU. Rajat Shubhra & Rahaman were standing motionless like a pillar."

"What happened? Was there any bad news?" I anxiously asked Mrityunjay babu.

"I was waiting anxiously outside the ICU. I noticed some of the

hospital staff & Sakilabanu were standing outside the ICU. Noticing me Sakilabanu rushing towards me started weeping in a gushing stream. Being astonished I asked her, 'Why so much crowd here?'

Sakilabanu while weeping replied, 'My loving Didi left us.'

Somebody started hammering within my heart. As I tried to enter the ICU, one nurse interdicted me to enter the ICU. She informed that the team of Cardiologists is trying hard to save the life of Kanaklata Devi.

I couldn't control myself. I rushed & sat on a chair kept outside with a thud. I started praying to God with folding hands for saving the life of Kanaklata.

But, that magnanimous Debi breathed last & left towards heaven making entire efforts futile."

Heart-rending grief suppressed so long comes down from the eyes of Mrityunjay babu as the stream of inundation of bursting cloud on hills. This stream of water is drifting away from all the congealed memories of the past. I being a listener of this glorious performance sit like an immovable pillar looking at the face of Mrityunjay babu. A few drops of tears roles down through my cheek imperceptibly.

I a silent, tranquil, immobile listener got back my senses from a sudden invocation of Mrityunjay babu, *"Sanjay babu, please come with me."*

"Where?" I ask being astonished.

"Let's move to that mausoleum of magnanimous lady."

Due to an imperceptible attraction, I go ahead at the heels of Mrityunjau babu.

Purchasing a fascicle of garland from a roadside flower shop, handing over a garland in my hand, he entered in a preserved garden adjoining the hospital. Along with me he comes & stands in front of a large white marbled alter.

Breaking his silence he says, *"This one is the mausoleum of that great Devi (Goddess)".*
I ask in inquisitiveness, *"Is this that place, where that great soul was dissolved into the five vital elements?"* Again in a continuous stream, the tears started rolling down from his eyes. In a choked voice he says, *"Yes, this is the place where her mortal body was cremated on a sandalwood funeral pyre. For that, her mausoleum was built here."*
I along with Mrityunjay babu offering the garland on the mausoleum make obeisance folding my hand towards that great soul.

I noticed that Mrityunjay babu sat in front of the mausoleum. A folding hand on the chest engages in meditation closing his eyes. I didn't want to interrupt his meditation. I felt internal that this old person how much used to love by heart his expired sister Kanaklata.

A thin deep black sheet of the evening is enveloping the entire area. Well decorated garden with illumination is sparkling. After a while, the old person's meditation is broken. The old ascetic getting up from trance says, *"Lets us go now Sanjay babu."*

Before exiting from the garden it comes to my view a tomb of black stone. I asked Mrityunjay babu, *"What's this? It seems to be a tomb. Whose grave is this one?"*
Mrityunjay babu halts. Taking me near the tomb he says, *"This one is the tomb of Sakila banu. After the expiry of Kanaklata, Sakila banu didn't live long. Her last wish was that after her death, she must be entombed near her beloved friend & sister Kanaklata."*

Folding my hand wishing her soul to be rest in peace, we came out of the garden.

The night was descending down. I will have to catch the local train to return to my home. I take leave of Mrityunjay babu holding his hands.

I was walking fast through the road towards the railway station. On the way, I turned back for a while. I looked back at the hospital behind. Raising head gloriously is thriving in the deep darkness well illuminated KANAKANJALI SUPER SPECIALTY HOSPITAL.

****

"Iti Shri Sanjay Ubaacha"

(Here concludes the narration of Shri Sanjay)